Waiting for Dinner or Death

To Jorma—
from a big, big fan.
[signature]
Dec. 6, 1997

See story p. 128

Waiting for Dinner or Death

Michael Leannah

NPI

Northwest Publishing, Inc.
Salt Lake City, Utah

NPI

Waiting for Dinner or Death

For information address: Brightside Publications
522 Grant Avenue, Sheboygan, WI 53081
920-457-4862

PRINTING HISTORY
First Printing 1996

ISBN: 1-56901-491-4

NPI books are published by Northwest Publishing, Incorporated,
6906 South 300 West, Salt Lake City, Utah 84047.
The name "NPI" and the "NPI" logo are trademarks belonging to
Northwest Publishing, Incorporated.

PRINTED IN THE UNITED STATES OF AMERICA.
10 9 8 7 6 5 4 3 2 1

To
Geralyn, Jacob, Willa, Sam,
Babe, Rascal, and the fish.

Look Out for Erskine

"Big Harry" Deale was blown apart in the foyer of his grand mansion on the outskirts of Louisville, his blood splattering the stucco, his guts spilling onto the floor like jellied cranberries sliding out of a can. The police counted 140 holes in all before scraping him into a plastic bag.

Big Harry's wife, Emily, doing her best to act distraught, told police her husband had excused himself from the breakfast table to answer the coded ring of the doorbell—two longs, three shorts, meaning it was one of his henchmen.

"It might have been someone named Erskine," she declared between sobs. "I heard him on the phone late last night, whispering sweet nothings to one of his thugs. 'Look out for Erskine,' he said. 'Whatever you do—look out for Erskine.'"

This lead kept the force occupied for three or four days, but it was all for nothing. 'Erskine' was Big Harry's name for any copper, and he finished all assignments with the directive, "Look out for Erskine."

They never found the killer, and it's just as well since Emily never reenacted her violence. She had no need to, as no one else jabbed her tender calves nightly with razor toenails.

Doctor's Orders

Past the maternity ward, down the hall to the left of intensive care, lies the busiest section of the Lewis Q. Soretoe Memorial Hospital: the hypochondriac ward, Dr. Oliver Severenjab presiding.

"Doctor, they've removed my appendix, but it *still* hurts!" wailed old Mrs. Gooseflesh.

"Doctor, do something!" Mr. Crank groaned. "The rash you said wasn't there is burning red and itching!"

"Doctor," cried Louise Fernstrom, after a sneezing fit. "Are you sure there are no more body parts I can have removed? I hurt all over."

"More medicine!" railed Joe Connundrum.

"Please do surgery again!" groaned Blanche LeBlanc.

Dr. Severenjab calmly made his rounds, a smile frozen on his lips, cotton firmly embedded in his ears.

He read the charts, took blood pressure readings, and checked reflexes, all the while humming "You Can't Always Get What You Want," in his usual carefree manner.

"What needs to be done, Doctor?" Nurse Watkins asked as the specialist removed his latex gloves and prepared to leave for lunch.

"The usual," Dr. Severenjab said firmly. "Send the bills out in time for the next postal pick-up."

#1 Draft Pick

It was almost kickoff time on a beautiful September Sunday afternoon. The Minnesota Vikings lined up to play the Green Bay Packers at Lambeau Field in Green Bay.

"Just think," Alphonso Merriweather Rotgut thought as he rose from his bleacher seat directly behind the Packers' bench. "All these people, thousands and thousands of them, all here to see me watch this football game."

He turned and waved to the cheering crowd. The game had begun.

Excitement for this game had been building for months. Not only was it the first game of a brand new season, it was the debut of the Packers' new kicker, Hans Derzeh.

Hans was the top player picked in the first round of the draft and with good reason. In college he regularly kicked field goals from as far away as 65 yards.

Adding fuel to the fire, Hans announced on draft day that his leg was getting stronger with time and he proved it by kicking 70- and even 80-yard field goals during practice. Now it was time to show what he could do in a real game, and the fans could hardly wait.

It wasn't just his ability to kick long field goals that intrigued the fans. It was his unusual method that brought the curiosity seekers out in droves.

They'd all seen kickers who used specially made shoes to kick field goals. There were even a few placekickers over the years who gained fame by kicking barefoot. Hans Derzeh kicked his field goals wearing an old Romeo slipper on his right foot.

"I don't know why it works," he told reporters on draft

day. "All I know is, my follow through gives me distance, and the Romeo slipper assures the accuracy."

He discovered the 'magical' Romeo slipper when he was still in high school. His brothers urged him to join them in a Sunday morning football game. Too lazy to get his shoes from upstairs, he slipped on his father's Romeo slippers, which were lying about in the front hall, as usual. The rest is history.

But, sadly, only that one particular right-foot Romeo slipper worked. When he tested his kick-offs using other Romeos, the results were execrable.

"My career will last only as long as the stitching in this Romeo slipper holds out," he confided once to his wife in intimate, late-night talk.

To his horror, on the day of the big game the coach's dog, Lombardi, who was allowed to sit on the sidelines with the players, chewed Hans's Romeo slipper to bits.

Wearing a regular shoe on his kicking foot, Hans missed field goals of 33, 36, 40, and 48 yards and, when the Packers scored a touchdown with two minutes remaining in the game, he missed the extra point. The Packers lost 51-6.

As the crowd booed loudly, Alphonso Merriweather Rotgut turned and waved to show his appreciation.

"Thank you for trying to help," he cried. "But save your breath. These fellows in the funny-looking helmets just won't sit down so I can see the game."

The JFK Story

I

"Jackie!" the maid shrieked. "Your date's been waiting nearly an hour!" She smiled nervously at the shy young man sitting on the arm of the couch.

"I'LL...BE...DOWN!" Jacqueline roared from her room at the top of the stairs. The maid grimaced. Jack's face turned red and he stared at his feet, wondering if he should have worn his brown shoes after all.

"Just because he's a congressman, who does he think he is?" Jackie snarled as she returned to her TV. Her knitted brow unfurled, her clenched jaw relaxed, a smile washed over her face. There on the screen was her true love, Fred Allen. She'd been listening to him on radio for years. Now she could see him on TV and her intestines were all aflutter.

Little did she know he wouldn't make it in television and her roving eye would be caught by other stage and screen personalities in the days and years to come, Tony Curtis and Dick Clark, to name just two.

As the credits rolled by at the end of the show, Jackie petulantly switched off the set. She placed a white pillbox on her head, fluffed her hair, and prepared to make her descent to her waiting beau.

II

In the hubbub after Jackie tossed her garter to the riffraff gathered at center stage, old friend Claudia Waterbubble sidled up to her.

"How are you, Jackie?" gushed Claudia.

"All I really want is to dance once with Teddy," Jackie confided before she was whisked away by her mother-in-law.

"Jack's such a bore," she thought through smiling teeth as he droned on at evening's end. "Always giving speeches, no matter where or what."

She was startled from her bitter musings when Jack turned to her, extended his hand, and said with impassioned oration, "So, Jackie, what I really want to say is, don't ask what your husband can do for you. Ask what you can do for your husband."

Jackie blushed as the room exploded with applause. Jack's speech writers scurried in all directions, trying to find a pen to write down what they knew was to be the catchphrase of the ages.

III

"...and the glow from that fire can truly light the world. And so, my fellow Americans...Ask not what you can do for your country, ask—"

"NO, NO, NO, NO, NO, NO, NO," the speech writers groaned, throwing their papers to the floor in disgust.

"Dammit, I did it again," Jack said angrily. "Let me try it once more. I'll get it right."

"Tomorrow's your inauguration, Jack," one of the writers warned. "Once and for all, cut the shit."

The president-elect shook his head despondently. Jackie smiled from the back of the room as if frozen, counting the hours until the next *American Bandstand.*

The Dawn and Death of the Teminterval

Ingqveld Johnson bitched and complained as he changed the bag on his vacuum cleaner, kicking up a cloud of dust in the process.

"There's just no end to the dust and dirt," he bemoaned. Then he added, "I just wish I hadn't been born a Norwegian."

If there was one thing Ingqveld Johnson couldn't stand, it was his Norwegian roots. Each day at least twice, once upon waking and again while brushing his teeth before bed, Ingqveld reminded himself of what little respect Norwegians garnered worldwide.

"We've never won a major war," he pointed out to himself as he dumped the old vacuum bag in the trash out back. "Not one famous leader or athlete. And they stick us way up by the Arctic Circle."

He was by now downright forlorn and bristling with nerve-ending whiplash. Later that afternoon though, inspiration came to him like a lover in the night.

Most human tasks, he reasoned, take longer than a minute but less than an hour. In other words, minutes and hours are often inadequate in communicating human needs. "I'll be back in a minute," usually means 15 or 20 minutes. And people are always splitting hours into halves or quarters.

In the interest of better human communication, Ingqveld Johnson developed the *teminterval,* short for "ten minute interval."

"People will get used to it," he said aloud as he picked lint off the rug excitedly. "'I'll be back in a teminterval.' 'The show will be over in two temintervals.' By God, I think I've got something here."

At first he wanted to call his new time units 'Ingqvelds,' but reconsidered, not wanting to appear vain. Temintervals, he decided, had a certain ring that would appeal to the masses.

But, as almost anyone could surmise, it never caught on, despite Ingqveld's impassioned proselytizing on radio and TV talk shows.

He remained an obscure Norwegian throughout his days, finally dying at age 74, in his own disgust.

The Wally Cox Memorial Barbecue and Reunion

There have to be more than eight people in the world named Wally Cox, but that's all that showed up at the 16th Annual Wally Cox Memorial Barbecue and Reunion, held

July 14, 1994, at Owls Head Park in Brooklyn, New York.

Participants at past events numbered as many as 36, in 1982, and as few as 6, in 1985. For those who show, it's always a grand time.

To be admitted, your name has to be Wally Cox, and you'd better have official proof. Imposters have tried to crash the event, but have always been discovered and dealt with accordingly.

The most famous person trying to pass himself off as a Wally Cox was former president Richard Nixon in 1980. Not many people know of Nixon's hero-worship of Wally Cox, the diminuitive, soft-spoken comic actor who died in 1973, at the height of his fame.

Desperate to attend the event, the former president disguised himself and participated in the reunion for over three hours before he was discovered by a Wally Cox from Dead Bird, Wyoming, who put two and two together when the newcomer rose and announced: "Let me say this, and I'll make it perfectly clear: Wally Cox was the greatest performer who ever lived, bar none!"

Nixon had been having the time of his life, smiling for the first time in ages, when he was banished from the picnic grounds. Major surgery had to be performed to get his face back to its usual length and dourness.

But who can blame him for enjoying himself? The Wally Cox Memorial Barbecue and Reunion was, for many, the event of the year. And every year the activities, guest speakers, and refreshments got better.

As was said, this year there were eight participants, all named Wally Cox. Here are the eight, from youngest to oldest:

Wally Cox, 10 months, of Whiteflat, Texas, son of Herman and Ethel Cox, school teachers. They always wanted to attend the Wally Cox reunion and were well aware of the rule that those under 16 were allowed to attend with guardians. They wasted no time naming their son appropriately.

Wally Cox, 22, of Wahoo, Nebraska, house painter. Comes dressed every year as Underdog, except once when ill and confused and came dressed as Tennessee Tuxedo.

Wally Cox, 31, of Mound Bayou, Mississippi, one-eyed, second string nose tackle for the Detroit Lions. Has caricature of Wally Cox tattooed on left biceps.

Wally Cox, 38, of Gila Bend, Arizona, computer analyst. Owns largest reported collection of Wally Cox memorabilia.

Wally Cox, 41, of Bird in Hand, Pennsylvania, used car salesman. Only participant to have met the famous Wally Cox, got his autograph while riding the same elevator in a New York hotel in 1963.

Wally Cox, 50, of Popham Beach, Maine, head librarian. Most frequent winner of the Wally Cox impersonation contest, is especially adept at imitating Wally Cox's dexterous whistling.

Wally Cox, 77, of Crivitz, Wisconsin, retired farmer. Comes every year even though he has no interest in the famous Wally Cox.

Wally Cox, 93, of Cooks Hammock, Florida, retired firefighter and potter. Once sold ceramic Wally Cox keychains at a reunion picnic—a big hit.

Before the festivities began, the formal meeting came to order. The Wally Cox from Popham Beach offered to invite to the next reunion a man he'd met who looked exactly like the famous Wally Cox. But, since the man's name was Arthur Delubre von Sconce, and not Wally Cox, he wouldn't be welcome (vote: 7-1), although photos of him would be gladly passed around, just for the hell of it.

A statute was clarified to state that a female member *would be* welcome, as long as her name was indeed Wally Cox. The Wally Cox from Wahoo related the story he'd heard of the Wally Cox fan who named his daughter Wally. Their last name was Dombrowski.

According to the story, the man was trying to help popularize Wally as a girl's name so more girls might be allowed into the annual reunion. Unfortunately, the man's farsightedness paid off in disappointment. The girl would have won a child's beauty pageant if not for her name. ("We can't have a winner named Wally Dombrowski!" shrieked the matronly old bag in charge.)

The guest speaker this year was Tony Randall himself, but most of the members were more interested in the videotapes of old *Mr. Peepers* and *Hiram Holiday* programs that the Wally Cox from Gila Bend was showing, so the speech was cut short.

The eight Wally Coxes got along very well in spite of a few minor problems. The baby cried throughout Tony Randall's speech, drawing looks of annoyance. And a small brawl broke out when the Wally Cox from Bird in Hand refused to stop crunching on celery with peanut butter during Wally's quips and witticisms on the *Hollywood Squares* tapes.

But once the activities started, everything was fine. The Wally Cox dance contest, the Wally Cox tobacco spit, and the look-alike and sound-alike contests were all well attended as usual.

A new event, the Wally Cox weight-lifting contest, was won by the Wally Cox who plays football for the Lions. There were no other entrants.

He also tried to pull off an upset in the look-alike contest. Weighing over 300 pounds, black, having only one eye, and sporting a grizzly beard, he hardly looked like the famous Wally Cox at all.

But he'd unearthed a little-known fact: Wally Cox had had six toes on his right foot. And, as if by a miracle, so did he. The judges fell over themselves to gaze at the quirky phenomenon, but they came to their senses at the last minute and awarded the prize to the baby, by virtue of his big ears and wide, stupid grin.

The festivities always include an extravagant chili dinner, due to an old rumor that chili had been Wally Cox's favorite food. Although this chili rumor has been conclusively disproved time and time again, the tradition remains.

The reunion ended with the members trading audio and video tapes of their hero's TV and movie performances. In this way, the members say, Wally Cox will live forever.

If your name is Wally Cox, look for upcoming information as to next year's reunion. Patricia Benoit is pegged to be the guest speaker, with a chance of a surprise appearance by Marlon Brando, who is invited every year to impart his reminiscences concerning his old pal, and yours, Wally Cox.

Proctologist's Progeny

Lester Miserables was a man destined to accomplish little in life. Living on an inheritance, he had time to explore details most of us wouldn't waste our time sneezing at.

Coin flipping fascinated him. He proved, by flipping individual coins 10,000 times each, that heavier dates influence the flight of a flipped coin. The face side of a 1988 quarter is heavier than that of a 1981 quarter, and will consequently land tails-up .0003% more often. Similarly, a 1988 penny will be tails .0007% more often than the 1911 make. This was just one of Lester's discoveries.

He would sit on his porch recording the number of cars passing by, categorizing them by make, color, number of passengers, whatever, and spend the afternoon drawing comparisons. Seeing as he lived on a lonely road on the outskirts of Wawa, Ontario, where usually not more than a handful of cars go by in a day, this was extremely tedious and unrewarding.

He would compare the number of Cheerios in the 24-ounce box to the number in the 32-ounce box and report to the company if he found a glaring discrepancy in the ratio. He made tally charts compiling data on everything from TV commercials to the junk mail he received every day.

"Leave him alone," next door neighbor Floyd Elise told his children, who wanted to tease and torment him. "His father was a proctologist who married a woman who'd been his patient."

Floyd Elise lowered his voice.

"It must be hell. How would you like to go through life knowing full well that you wouldn't exist on earth had it not been for an aggressive case of anal warts?"

Over the Hill and Far Away

"I never thought I'd be what I am today—35 and fat," said Warren Vietnam. Being a former high school athlete who'd lettered in football and track, it was indeed surprising.

"It's better than being 38 and fat," said his friend Laslo Beltloop. "And anyway, at least you have memories of being thin."

Laslo had always been envious of his lifelong friend Warren. Laslo had never known the glories of being a stand-out athlete in high school, of entertaining the notion of continuing sports in college, of being able to sit in taverns ever after, reminiscing.

And it wasn't that Laslo lacked the nerve. He tried out for football one year, but quit when the coach yelled at him for not catching a pass thrown low and wide.

"Die for it!" the coach screamed with rattling teeth. Laslo said, "Screw you," under his breath and quit.

Years later, while rolling awake in the middle of the night, it dawned on him that what the coach had yelled was "Dive for it!"

But it was too late to do anything about it now, and they don't have football leagues for overweight suburbanites, so his dreams of glory were never to be.

All In, Down Under

Cornelius Yibbleyabble made the terrible mistake of saying he was lonely in a letter to his mother. "Since I left Ann (that nagging dog in heat)," he wrote, "I don't know which way to turn."

His mother wrote back. "Son, you don't need to be lonely. Your sister Evie, your little nephew Crudd, and I will be driving to Newark this weekend to attend a bingo festival at Evie's ex-husband's church. You can join us." This was hardly possible, as Cornelius was now living in Australia.

He had no skills and nothing else to do, so he put a notice in the Australian Yellow Pages advertising himself as a private detective. "I specialize in hard-to-solve mysteries," his ad read. It included a silhouetted profile of Sherlock Holmes.

In a matter of weeks his track record was zero for twenty-three. When at last someone vociferously complained, Cornelius struck a Sherlock-like pose and sneered, "I *said* I specialize in hard-to-solve mysteries. And these have been nearly impossible, at least for the likes of me."

Despite his lack of success and charisma, the young woman next door took a liking to him and named her baby after him. Yibbleyabble Valhalla Vellella-van Jones later became a high ranking official in Australian internal affairs.

Before the kangaroo milk scandal did him in, the people loved him far and wide. Even after the scandal a few continued to love him, namely his wife and kids, and that's all he really needed in the first place.

The Resolutions of I. Wilhelm Sneever

I. Wilhelm Sneever was resting quietly in his garden when all of a sudden he sat bolt upright and made a vow.

"I, I. Wilhelm Sneever, vow to cease munching the toasties and gaining fat weight," he said aloud, causing the garden to fritter. He further commented.

"I, I. Wilhelm Sneever, vow to cease teasing and nagging my wife, Julia Sneever, seeing as she's been dead for seven years and can no longer hear me anyway."

He fidgeted in his seat as if small electric shocks were taking place.

"I vow to cease placing long-distance telephone calls to total strangers, pretending to be a pollster, and asking nosy questions."

The sky was clear, but clouds drifted over the old man's thoughts momentarily, then lifted again.

"I vow to sit on my chairs on a rotational basis so they wear out at the same rate."

He was trembling now and salivating. This was resolution-making with a vengeance.

"I, I. Wilhelm Sneever, vow to cease second-guessing and verbally haranguing the meteorologists on the ten o'clock news each night.

"I vow to cease gazing at my neighbor lady's undergarments when they're hung on the clothesline on Tuesdays.

"I vow to cease playing my ukulele at picnics after people ask me to stop."

His mind slowed almost to a halt, like a runaway army tank finally rolling to a stop.

"I vow to speak more clearly in my dreams at night so people can understand me. That way I won't awaken each morning utterly frustrated and fit to be tied."

This he mumbled as he drifted into sleep in his garden.

Irene Fist, Teacher Extraordinaire

It was lunch time at Pangborn Elementary School in

Levittown, New York. As the kids whooped it up outside on the playground, Mrs. Irene Fist sat numb in the teachers' lounge, gumming down a tunafish sandwich with great difficulty. She'd had better years and her age was showing badly.

Mr. Bownsem, the gym teacher, jabbed vicious pins into the tiny voodoo dolls he kept lined up on the wall next to the bulletin board. Labeled 'Jimmy,' 'Lori,' 'Stevie,' 'Billy,' etc., the dolls had been made by the students of his wife, Grace, home ec teacher at the nearby high school.

"Take that, you little son of a bitch," he wheezed as he punctured a doll labeled 'Ricky.' Mrs. Fist smiled, distracted momentarily from the heavy thoughts brought on by the morning news.

Two of her former students, Egmund Feenabottom Soupstain and David Schnitzelweiner, had been found dead, the result of an alleged suicide pact.

Mrs. Fist fondly remembered the two, though it had been 15 years since their eighth grade graduation. Academically they hadn't been much but they were two of her most remarkable students nonetheless.

When Egmund Feenabottom Soupstain first entered her classroom as an eight year old second grader, Mrs. Fist noted immediately the child's strong resemblance to Miles Davis—skin as black as night, large curious eyes, close-cropped hair, and a quiet air of confidence bordering on arrogance.

Minutes later, in walked David Schnitzelweiner, a deadpan look on his face, a bored, lazy shuffle of a stroll, and a face featuring beady eyes, flabby jowls, and a receding hairline. The resemblance to David Brinkley was simply uncanny.

Knowing they were destined for greatness, Mrs. Fist gave them preferential treatment throughout the year and followed their progress as they grew and developed.

She'd been mildly surprised to hear that at age eighteen, Egmund Feenabottom Soupstain had enrolled in the state university to study broadcast journalism, while David Schnitzelweiner was slated to study music at Julliard.

They each made it big in their respective careers. Egmund changed his name to Alan Jones and was hired on as anchorman at a TV station in Detroit.

David Schnitzelweiner, looking more like David Brinkley every day, entertained crowds in the hippest nightspots in New York, blowing trumpet warm and clear, into the night and up to the stars.

The trouble began when Egmund was hired by a news station in New York. The two were together again and their love affair blossomed into a fiery, thorn-studded rose.

Every night after the news, Egmund sought out David and his jazz and passed the hours waiting for him to finish. They'd retire to Egmund's apartment on Washington Square for lovemaking and what-not.

And each night they parted the same way: David would turn at the door and say, "Good night, Egmund." And Egmund would say, "Good night, David," and then, after David left, he'd turn to the window and, pretending it was a TV monitor, Egmund, whose idol had always been Chet Huntley, would say with the utmost seriousness, "And good night from NBC News." He'd then go off to bed.

This was confusing to the deaf girl across the way who secretly watched through a high powered telescope as Egmund and David made love each night. She could read lips with the best of them and, being too young to remember the Huntley/Brinkley sign-off routine, couldn't for the life of her imagine why in the world Egmund would say such a thing after saying goodbye to his lover.

No one knows why they jumped from the bridge together. Mrs. Fist sat and despondently pondered as Mr. Bownsem stabbed needles into voodoo dolls.

Mrs. Fist (whose own children—Albert, Edna, Ignatius, Olive, and Ulysses, from her current marriage, and Yves, of whom she shared custody with her first husband—gave her enough headaches to last a person a lifetime) thought about her present brood of second graders. There were always at least a couple who bore likeness to the famous.

This year she had Roy Wrolfstadt, who, with his barrel-like trunk, wide flat nose, and slicked-back hair, was the spittin' image of Babe Ruth himself. Sadistically, she kept him in for recess more often than not.

And every time she laid eyes on Dickie Veebelfester, she saw Pat Boone. Mrs. Fist couldn't stand Pat Boone, so whenever Dickie raised his hand in class, she ignored him and moved on to the next subject.

Then there was Molly Nesbitt-Crisp, Ma Barker incarnate, ornery demeanor, perpetual scowl, penchant for bossing the boys, bad haircut, and all.

Mr. Diddlysquat, the principal, suddenly burst in, bitched at them all with a vengeance, then retreated to his office for more daydreaming.

Mrs. Irene Fist trudged back to her classroom to straighten out the mess she'd started.

The Collection of Wiley Klontz

Wiley Klontz had been a good little boy and he grew to be a good little man. If only his mother could have realized.

"Mama," little three year old Wiley once asked. "Is Sirius in the constellation of Orion or in the constellation of Canis Major?"

"Canis Major," she mumbled as she wolfed down another doughnut.

"I couldn't remember," he said.

"Nobody ever said you were bright," she spat.

Wiley grew up in the suburbs of Detroit, where as a man, he found himself toiling away in the auto industry, working his way up the corporate ladder until he was made head designer for the Ford Motor Company.

His "baby" was a heavy, bull-like car that, with the roof

flipped back, converted into a type of pick-up truck. It was capable of carrying heavy loads through any terrain.

Throughout the months of planning he'd called it the "Ford Workman" but by the time of its public unveiling, the name had been changed to the catchy "Ford Laborer."

His reputation suffered an agonizing death when it was discovered that the car was too heavy to climb most hills.

By the year 2025, Wiley Klontz was living out his life quietly and harmlessly in northern Minnesota. He found himself doing such things as saving plastic bags, pieces of foil, and old jars. At first he kept his collection in a kitchen cupboard but when it began to overflow he had to use the shelves in the basement.

"Thank God my father lived through the Great Depression and told me all about it every step of the way," he remarked, using keen insight. "It gives me a ready-made excuse for my quirky behavior here now in old age."

Thinking back on times when he'd needed a rubber band or a paper clip and didn't have one handy, Wiley Klontz quoted his father for the umpteenth time that day: "You never know when you might need something."

Wiley suffered a stroke at age 80 that rendered him useless in a hospital bed for months. After he died, his grown children came to his house to pick his bones clean. Any and all of his belongings were promptly carted away.

But no one wanted his collection. It gathered dust for months, which is what it had been doing when Wiley was alive.

The house was eventually sold, Louis and Eugenia Harrigan moved in, and the collection was thrown into the trash without the least bit of fanfare. And the ghost of Wiley Klontz was irate.

"Where are my jars?" the Harrigans heard at night. "Where are the plastic bags? I want my alooooooominum!"

They had to retrieve the mountain of junk and put it back on the shelves in the basement before the ghost of Wiley

Klontz would leave them alone. But now they had a new problem.

Louis's mother, Wiltilda Harrigan, complained loudly about the junk in the basement. "My son never had to live with such clutter when he lived at home," she said angrily.

Eugenia, who'd been getting sick of her mother-in-law anyway, nailed the old woman between the eyes with a broomstick and buried her in a crawlspace behind a basement wall.

Now the Harrigans are treated to nightly shouting matches between the ghost of Wiltilda Harrigan and the ghost of Wiley Klontz.

"I want this garbage removed from here immediately!"

"Over my dead body! You never know when you might need a jar or a scrap of foil!"

On and on it went. The Harrigans got used to it. And they never did get rid of the junk.

Louis was finally getting back at his mother after all these years.

Death of a Patriarch

At long last, Hans Gerber was dead. The founder of Gerber Baby Foods drew his last breath at 11:10 p.m. on December 14, 1986. He was ninety-eight years old.

His solemn family surrounded his deathbed mumbling prayers and epithets. Then they ordered out for hamburgers.

"No more strained peaches," said his son Herb.

"No more stewed prunes," said Margaret, his youngest granddaughter.

"No more mushed zucchini," said his son-in-law Clarence.

"No more having to find new disposal sites for all those little jars," said Emma, his wife.

As per Hans Gerber's implicit directions, the body was

strained and vacuum-sealed in 4-ounce jars. All 108 of them were placed in a vault and buried on a hillside in Pennsylvania, where thousands of babies come to pay homage each year.

When Shadows Run Rampant

"Oh, pardon me," he said as he backed into the endtable, making the flowers in the vase shake. Later he tripped and stumbled into the coat tree by the front door. "Excuse me," he said to the coats hanging there like dead fish on a silver stringer.

Paying his penance as always, Carl Jung excused, pardoned, and apologized his way through another day.

A very decent fellow whose microbes tingled upon hearing himself described as "nice," Carl bumbled through each day intent on one thing: To get through the day without giving in to his sexual desires.

He was born with a swarm of them but someday he'd be out of this life, reincarnated into someone with a new batch of shortcomings and desires, so his mission was to get to Judgment Day without any black marks, without giving in to his dreadful, debased fantasies.

His parents had higher hopes for him. They'd named him with the hope that he'd become a great psychological-scientific mind. Or at least a doctor. In reality, he sold vacuum cleaners door to door and tuned pianos in the evenings, all the while enduring his lust for life.

"I'm awfully sorry," he said to the pillow he dropped on the floor as he arranged things just so before crawling in for the night. This was the best time of day for Carl. It meant he'd gotten through another series of urges and temptations intact.

Sometimes, on days when shadows run rampant, he tucks himself in as early as three o'clock in the afternoon and clings to the hope that the morning will find him in control once more.

"Sometimes I wish I'd never been born," he once said. And he was right.

The Jesus Question

Jose Schrempf never cared for religion, least of all as a child when they made him go to church. His life turned in a different direction one Saturday night though, when he stayed up late watching TV and eating pizza. While switching channels, he came upon a program that was to become the foundation of his new life.

There, haranguing anyone who would tune in, was Neil Downalot, TV evangelist and master con man. Mr. Schrempf was transfixed for the next sixty minutes.

The Reverend Downalot repeatedly asked the question that would burn in the ears of Jose Schrempf from that night onward:

"What would Jesus do?"

Jose Schrempf responded by calling 1-900-DIGDEEP to pledge monthly donations he couldn't afford. And the following morning he walked the streets in search of ways to serve the Almighty. He scrounged the gutters and alleyways and found a collection of beings wasted and bleeding, teeth a-chatter and minds adrift.

Driven by The Jesus Question, which burned in his consciousness like a red hot poker in solidified grease, Jose Schrempf led his disciples toward a steeple in the distance. Soon they were climbing the marble steps of the Church of Our Lady of Agony (and Lesser Discomforts). Mr. Schrempf marched his band of converts up to the massive doors.

The Sunday service had just begun when the group scuffled in, some coughing, some wheezing, all looking around in a daze. Mr. Schrempf led them up the center aisle and was about to usher them into a pew, when the pastor, Rev. Randolph Queelacoogin Longtongue came running all over himself, cassock billowing, scapular flying. Bishop Alonzo Littlenoodle was in attendance and he, too, rushed to the scene.

"What are you doing here?" Rev. Longtongue hissed through his teeth, ugly veins in his neck protruding like wire cables in an electrical hotbox.

"This is the house of the Lord," Jose Schrempf declared.

"Get the hell out of here!" barked the bishop, whose miter fell to the floor in the bargain.

Jose Schrempf led his sad lot out into the cruel world again as Rev. Longtongue looked for the custodian to mop up the floor after them.

The organ groaned, the congregation hung their heads, the collection baskets were passed, the priest swilled the wine.

And out on the sidewalk, bitter winds howled. Saliva froze on the chins of the ragged. Spires and steeples rose from the city skyline, trying to puncture the low-hanging, overcast sky.

All That Cacophony

There were many things that attracted Pablo Dali to New Orleans: the climate, the restaurants, the rich and wonderful history. For years he'd thought about moving there but once he did, he immediately realized he'd made a terrible mistake. He forgot he hated jazz.

Every night he'd stand at his window looking down with a sneer as street musicians congregated like unwanted rodents. Later he'd roll in the sheets with a pillow over his head, trying to block out the cacophonous onslaught.

The police grew sick of him calling and waking them up at all hours of the night. “If you hate jazz so much, why do you live on Bourbon Street?” demanded Sgt. Burly Dicque, a vague relation of Jack Teagarden himself.

One night, at the dead of dawn, Pablo, who at four A.M. had finally fallen into a rocky garden of fitful sleep, was awakened by a glimmering light. Peering closely, he could see the faint outline of a body.

“Hello, Pablo,” the glowing ghost said in a raspy, gravelly voice. “This is Louis, Pablo.”

“Huh?”

“Louis. Louis Armstrong.”

“What is it? What do you want?”

“I hear you don’t like the music.”

“I’m-I’m sorry,” Pablo stammered. “I can’t stand it. Don’t be angry with me.”

“I’m not angry,” Louis assured him. “I hated it at first, too. It’s loud, hard to follow, has no beginning, middle, or end. Especially this Dixieland crap you get around here. I had to read the reviews in the paper all the time to know who was good and who was bad at it.

“But it’s where the money is. If people wanted to pay me for honking on a horn, then that’s what I was going to do. If you smile a lot, they keep coming back, and if they keep coming back, it gets easier to smile.”

The next day, Pablo Dali rented the storefront below and opened Armstrong’s Restaurant, named to honor the great musician whose spirit inspired its creation. He was soon raking in money hand over fist.

In his old age Pablo Dali had more money than any ten people in New Orleans. He retired and did what he’d been wanting to do all along. He formed the Anti-Jazz Society.

In another city, he would have had some takers. But this was New Orleans. Nobody hates jazz in New Orleans.

Or if they do, they won’t admit it.

Having Fifi for Lunch

She marched up the street with a vengeance, her mink stole flapping in the wind. She spied her destination and quickened her angry pace. With heels clicking and jaw muscles working madly, she strode to the entrance like the matronly old bag that she was.

She was Beatrice Oops and the store she entered was Necks and Pets, combination meat market and pet shop.

"I'd like to buy another obnoxious little dog," she growled. "Nothing is better for keeping my husband's wretched relatives from visiting."

"What happened to the last one, Mrs. Oops?" asked store owner Butch Cronkite, using his apron to wipe blood from his hands.

"Never mind," Beatrice said with a snarl, not wanting to admit it had run off with the dog of some common people up the street.

Filled with delight and tickled beyond compare, Beatrice left the store with another overgrown rat on a string, only to realize upon her arrival home that she was too late.

Her husband's brother, his wife, and their sixteen kids had already made themselves comfortable. Their Great Dane had little Fifi for lunch.

Suburbanite's Saga

Kevin Whitebelly had never been so embarrassed. He'd put his trash at the curbside on the wrong night and didn't realize his mistake until well after most of his neighbors probably saw it.

He lived in the suburbs, which was an accomplishment by itself. But Kevin could also brag that his was the best-tended lawn on Cement Devastation Circle in Plowed-Over Valley,

New Jersey, just this side of Paterson. Unfortunately for him, as anyone with a lawn fetish will tell you, enough is never enough.

For people like Kevin Whitebelly yardwork is never finished. He lived for his yardwork. He looked forward to vacations so he could groom the turf with no time constraints or external demands.

Kevin hadn't always been this way. In fact, he paid silent homage every day of his suburban life to his old neighbor, Floyd Ubunk, who once took it upon himself to draw Kevin aside, put his arm around his shoulder, and say, "Son, just look at the condition of your lawn…," proceeding to instruct him in the fine art of lawn maintenance and foolish pride.

Kevin Whitebelly lifted weights in winter so he'd be in tiptop shape for lawn mowing in the spring. He could mow one-handed, with a manual, *non*-self-propelled mower!

To be fair, it must be said that Kevin loved all forms of yardwork, not just mowing, although mowing was indeed his ultimate passion. But be it raking, weeding, turf-building, edging or what-have-you, Kevin Whitebelly did it with pomp and pride, all the while whistling "I Get the Blues When It Rains."

As with most lawn and yard nuts, Kevin had his collection of sayings, stories, and witticisms that Ventreblanc, his wife, collected for the express purpose of being read at his funeral. These are some of the random quotes recorded by Ventreblanc Whitebelly:

"What this country needs is a good ten-dollar lawn edger."

"Look at that asshole Dickens across the street, leaving his grass clippings in the gutter again. He needs a mulcher bad!"

"Raking leaves is a lot like life: You're never finished until you die."

"Paradise is a charge card and unlimited browsing time in a seed and fertilizer store."

"Dandelions are God's reminder that hell exists on Earth."

It is indeed true, by the way, that at the age of seventeen, Kevin Whitebelly said at a YMCA gathering, "One man's weed is another man's wildflower, you know," much to his everlasting shame. Unfriendly acquaintances brought this up from time to time just to watch him bristle.

Nothing made this man so happy as spreading turf builder on the sod, making the grass grow like hell so he could cut it down to size next Saturday.

And he'd be happy still to this day if he hadn't died on February 18, 1991, impaling himself on the handle of a snow shovel in a freak accident while cleaning out the garage.

Johnny Quickly

Mercifully, John Quickly died in his sleep last night. At last he is at rest.

While of this earth, he never once was able to slow down or relax. It was always one thing after another, as far as he was concerned. Life was one long series of crises.

"Johnny Quickly, take the garbage out before you leave," his mother would yell in the morning.

"Johnny Quickly, come up and get your report card," his teacher said.

"Johnny Quickly, report to my office," said the boss.

"John Quickly, come and claim the prize you won on today's radio program."

"John Quickly, your dishwasher is ready to be picked up from our repair department."

"John Quickly, here are your X-rays. The doctor will be with you shortly."

For this poor man, frantic was a way of life. We can only hope that his just reward is a call from the heavenly Father above: "John Quickly, come and sit at my right hand."

A Doctor's Dilemma

Ordinary old walk-of-life-type people don't know this, but most doctors mull over deep, vexing questions on their way to work each morning, and often on the drive home later as well.

"Should I advise Mrs. Ingeldinger to have the operation on her sluggish liver, or should we take a chance on the new medication just in from the labs?"

"Could Mr. Oswald Snitty have been saved after all if I'd realized immediately that the lump in the area of his bladder had been a small tumor and not a prune pit he'd swallowed, as I first diagnosed?"

"Will I ever feel the time is right to leave the clinic, go into research, and discover the cure for cancer?"

For Dr. Eugene W. Bedsore, it was different. As he fought the traffic on his way to work one summer's morning, the persistent question burning at the forefront of his consciousness was: *How in the hell am I ever going to be able to afford that fur coat Grace wants for her birthday?*

Indeed, it was a problem. His wife Grace had a birthday coming in ten days and Dr. Bedsore had lost his socks at the racetrack last weekend when she thought he was in Peoria visiting his sick aunt.

"I guess I could overcharge Mrs. Groundswell this afternoon," he mused. "How would she ever know the difference? Oh, but Miss Sluttishly, my secretary and accountant, would find out. Damn that meddling witch!" He was so angry he didn't even see the light change to red, and he sped right through as if no one else in the world existed.

"I suppose I could practice on my own, after hours," he thought. "That storeroom in the basement could be fixed up. But then Grace would get suspicious. Damn it all."

His worries were all for naught. Later in the afternoon he hit it big on a lottery ticket, taking home a tidy bundle and a mink for Grace, both of which he hid in the hall closet under the medical supplies he'd been filching from the office.

Grace was one step ahead of him though.

"Gene, you never went to Peoria, did you? You were at the race track again, weren't you?"

"How did you know?" the defeated man asked wearily.

"I've been counting your socks before and after your trips," she said. And with that she let him have it with the mop handle, the way she used to in the early days of their marital bliss, before he'd hit it big as a doctor.

Custer's Second-Last Stand

The sun was high. The horses tied to the mess wagon kicked up a cloud of dust as they whisked their tails at pesky flies.

General Custer sat on a log, took off his hat and wiped the sweat from his brow. The men were about to dig in to their dinners when the cook appeared, looking dejected.

"We're out of water," he said unhappily.

"Whose turn is it to fetch the damn water?" Custer asked without looking up.

"It's yours," said Corporal Sanborn, a young, undisciplined upstart. The other men stirred uneasily.

"What'd you say?" the general said with a scowl.

"I said it's your turn to fetch the water," Sanborn said without hesitation. "The men aren't going to run and fetch for you anymore until you take your rightful turn yourself."

"The men?" Custer murmured, his eyes scanning the faces that surrounded him.

"That's right, sir," said Sergeant Fulbright. "We told you back in Skunkfoot that we expect you to take your share of the everyday duties around here."

"And as you will certainly recall," Custer said with a sneer, "I told all of you that as general and big cheese of this outfit I won't be cowed into doing any of the menial labor."

"It's your turn, sir," said Sanborn icily.

"I simply refuse," Custer answered peevishly, crossing his arms in stubbornness. A collective grumble from the soldiers was split by the quiet voice of the cook.

"I can't make peanut butter fudge without water," he said with a helpless shrug of the shoulders.

"You have all the other ingredients?" Custer asked grimly.

The cook nodded.

Custer glared at the men. "You all want peanut butter fudge, don't you?"

"Not as bad as you do," said Sanborn. The men knew they had him where they wanted him. Custer's face turned red. He gritted his teeth.

"I ain't going," he said.

"I says you are," Sanborn said bravely.

"Corporal Sanborn, I'll remind you that you are a soldier of the U.S. Army and that you will take orders from me," the general said uncertainly.

"I'll take orders from you concerning strategies of battle but I didn't sign on with Uncle Sam to fetch your gol-durn water," Sanborn said with resolve. Then, a little confused, he said, "Wait a minute. Is the term 'Uncle Sam' in use yet, or does it come later in history?" No one paid any attention.

The argument dragged on. The soldiers knew the general was fighting from a feeble position. Since they'd set out from Missouri nearly a month ago, the general had eaten peanut butter fudge with every meal. They knew he had a tremendous weakness for it and probably wouldn't be able to hold out for long.

"I can go without water—AND peanut butter fudge—just as long as any of you," Custer said. "And when we get back to Washington, hell is gonna fly. Just you wait."

"I say he's bluffing," Sanborn snarled. "He says he can hold out, but we've all seen him at chow time. I say he can't go without peanut butter fudge for more than a day."

"I'm not the only one who likes peanut butter fudge," Custer rejoined. "All of you men have had it with your meals too. And we're damn lucky to have us a cook who knows how to whip up a batch of it at a moment's notice, especially seeing that peanut butter ain't really been officially invented yet."

"I'll get the water on one condition," a wizened old scout named Bailey blurted. He waited for silence before nervously expressing his proposal.

"The men have been looking at you, General," he said. "And we've been away from our wives and womenfolk an awful long time. You've got that long golden hair. Hell, from behind you look like my dear old Marthy when she was just a lass."

"What are you saying?" asked the horrified Custer.

"I'll run and get the water, if you'll just put on a petticoat and let us chase you around a little. It'll do us all good."

General Custer adamantly refused to comply with the request, shuddering at the thought of what would befall him if they were to catch him under those circumstances.

Curses and jeers stirred the regiment when all at once a messenger arrived with an urgent notice for General George. Custer ripped the paper from the messenger's hand and read it with a sour look on his face.

"Well, men," he said gravely. "Indians have been sighted not far from here, up on the banks of the Little Bighorn. This is what we've come for."

The men rose with a clatter of weapons and a thicket of dust. Falling into formation, they pulled in their reins and waited for instructions from the general.

"Men, let's put our differences aside for the time being and make this short and sweet. We should be finished by sundown. But let me make it clear right here and now: I won't be the one to fetch the damn water when we come back."

With that, he spurred his horse and galloped into the sage.

Biding Time, As Usual

Slipshod Ramshackle and his wife Yolanda lay in bed on a Tuesday morning, neither having the desire or the energy to get up for work.

"What do you want for breakfast, dear?" Yolanda asked through a wide yawn.

"Don't matter," Slipshod replied, unshaven.

"Is this the day your secretary is out?" she asked, trying to keep the conversation alive.

"That's tomorrow," he answered, scratching himself in places too dark to mention.

"What's on your agenda today?" she sighed.

"I don't know," he said. "I'm just biding my time till the weekend gets here." He swallowed some of last night's spaghetti that he'd vomited up during the night, giving it further consideration.

"Seems in general I'm just biding my time until I retire," he moaned. "O' course after I retire, I'll just die anyway probably."

The rest of the day, and the rest of his life, went on in this fashion.

Sitting in the Living Room with Nothing On

"I'm Hoyle Winkerman and welcome to *Celebrity Interviews.* On tonight's show we have with us porno movie stud, Big Johnny Stallion.

"Big Johnny, don't you sometimes feel funny being in such movies? I mean, don't you ever think of your mother, or grandma, or your little nieces and nephews, while you're stroking and squelching away for all the world to see?"

"Well, Hoyle, I used to. But my career turned around the night I had a heart-to-heart with my co-star in *Cream Dreams*, Big Wanda Bazoomba, who I'll always be indebted to.

"She said, 'Johnny,' she said. She said, 'You've got to use what the good Lord gives you. Not everyone has a 78-inch bust like mine. And, heaven knows, not all men are built like you.'

"So, Hoyle, what I'm saying is, I'm just trying to use the gifts the Lord has given me, and—"

CLICK!

"Diet-Mania brings you another delicious way to lose weight—fast!

"Introducing the new Diet-Mania Nutty Turtle Fudge Caramel Cashew Marshmallow Sundae, with only 90% of the calories of a regular Nutty Turtle Fudge Caramel Cashew Marshmallow Sundae.

"Made with real soy powder ice cream and low-cal imitation marshmallow, your family will agree—"

CLICK!

"Stay tuned for the premier of the smash-hit comedy *Total Strangers*.

"When Rod Brown, a single father, loses his son in a car accident, he fights to adopt three boys of different cultural backgrounds. Before they are able to set up a household, Rod discovers he has brain cancer.

"On his deathbed, he asks his girlfriend Julia to take care of the boys. Julia, who was adopted herself as an infant, is suddenly visited upon by her long-lost mother, now 68 and aging rapidly.

"Julia is crushed by a falling scaffolding and the boys—Mohammed, a refugee from war-torn east-Africa, Cabu, a homeless waif from Pakistan, and Manuel, an urchin from the mean streets of Rio de Janeiro—are left with Julia's mother.

"Can a slightly alcoholic elderly woman raise a trio of rough-and-tumble boys when the four have absolutely nothing in common?

"Be sure to tune in to the hilarious—"

CLICK!

"Thank you, everybody, and welcome to *'Laugh Tracks'*, the show where the studio audience is divided into competing sections and called upon to produce spontaneous laughter for skits performed on our stage, none of which are guaranteed to be funny.

"Our first skit tonight—"

CLICK!

"Tonight on *Suicide: 911,* you will see actual footage of despondent people about to take their lives. Our roving reporter, Kent Butterworth, will once again be on the scene at death's door, to try to pull them through."

CLICK!

"This is as good a night as any to start another baby boom," said Phil and Georgia Rosenbloom in unison.

A Tale of Two Biddies

Agnes Penelope Dishpan removed the last cushion from the couch and, holding her breath, probed the crack for loose change. None. She retrieved a pen and two lipstick dispensers, but no money.

Her roommate Virginia Creek entered, her wrinkled puss contorting into what a prune would look like if left soaking overnight in lemon juice.

"Agnes, you've gone through that couch three times already this afternoon," she spat. "What in hell's name are you trying to do?"

"I'm hoping to find money, if it's any damn business of yours," Agnes barked like a snarling wild dog. "I'm in arrears to that lousy, no-good son of mine."

"How much do you owe him?" Virginia snapped.

"Seventy-five dollars," Agnes bitched.

Virginia shook her head in disgust and made for the kitchen, unable to stand the sight of her roommate any longer.

The words of her late husband Fud, a sick-minded misogynist, rang in her ears as she mixed her instant coffee. He'd been a zoology professor at the university and had once told Virginia that putting two male Siamese fighting fish together in the same aquarium was like putting two female octogenarians in the same room.

"They'll tear each other apart," Virginia remembered him saying, as she brushed breadcrumbs from the tabletop.

Virginia blew on her drink, clicking her fingernails nervously under the table. She looked down at her purple bathrobe, noticing splotches and stains. It had been days since she'd gotten dressed.

Today was Thursday, and Virginia had gotten up as she always did on Thursdays—wishing it were Friday. Presently, Agnes burst into the kitchen, her words aflit and aflutter.

"Virginia," she said with a hissing enthusiasm. "I've thought of a way to raise the seventy-five dollars!"

"What?" the old woman asked, though she'd undoubtedly heard, "How?"

"Well," Agnes explained. "Between the two of us, how much money do we lose in the cushions of the couch? Not much at all. And why? Because we carry our money in our purses. Who carries loose change in their pockets and loses it in couches and davenports? Men."

Virginia didn't follow Agnes, but that was nothing new.

"So!" Agnes continued, her excitement clearly showing. "To get money, we need to invite some men over, have them sit on the couch, and after they leave, comb the cracks for coins. I tell you it can't miss."

The gleeful woman danced a jig of joy right there and then, in full view of the parakeet in the cage in the corner. Virginia was doubtful but there was no stopping Agnes now.

The first victim was Mr. Wilbur Schnark, retired meat cutter and long-time neighbor of the larcenous ladies. Suspicious beyond all belief (having never been invited over before in all the 34 years he'd lived there), the poor man left in a rush with Agnes howling at him for not dropping any change.

"We should have known better," she spat in disgust. "The old chiseler doesn't carry money when he leaves the house."

They were encouraged when the mailman sat for a spell the next day, eating a crumpet or two. Sure enough, he left a quarter behind in the couch cushions, as well as two 20 cent stamps.

"We're improving," Agnes said as she dropped the booty into a teapot above the stove.

Virginia, being an inveterate flirt, went along with Agnes's plan whole-heartedly. Her conscience nagged at her for scrounging money from a bunch of tired old schlemiels, but what the hell. The opportunity to speed up a man's heartrate by batting her eyelashes didn't present itself often anymore, and she liked the challenge.

Agnes suggested that more loose change would find its way into the couch cracks if the men were coaxed into a horizontal position. One thing led to another and soon the two of them were unabashedly seducing any men with jingling pockets.

"Can't we go into the bedroom?" asked shy Mr. Overblatt.

"No," Agnes breathed in his ear. "There's something about the couch I like."

It took them almost a year to raise the seventy-five dollars, which is a lot of money in nickels, dimes, and quarters. They didn't want to stop.

"If we can save up $29.95, we can finally send in for a Veg-o-matic," cackled Agnes. Virginia couldn't have agreed more.

Baby's First Words

"Say da-da!" Moses Furpo implored the newborn infant. The rough and craggy man cradled the tiny baby in his big, hairy arms. "Say da-da!"

The baby, Brutus, rolled his eyes and squirmed.

"He can't say any words yet," scolded Moses's wife, Elijalina.

Moses growled at her, shaking the baby gently, trying to coax it out of him.

Every day for months Moses shouted and cajoled and begged and pleaded for the baby to say 'da-da.' Nothing had ever been so important to him.

Then one dark day shortly before his first birthday, Brutus looked up at his parents with smiling eyes and said something that sounded like "Why me?" Obviously nothing more than a coincidental quirk of verbiage, Moses and Elijalina laughed quietly.

Later, Elijalina insisted on listing 'Why me?' in Brutus's baby book as his first words, leading Moses to demand a messy divorce.

Ninety-three years later, Brutus Furpo uttered, 'Why me?' before gently falling into his eternal sleep.

George Bush's Last Twenty Minutes in the White House

Outside the oval office, down a rarely used hallway that leads to a cluster of small meeting rooms, there is an unmarked door that appears to be painted shut.

It's a small room, barely big enough to accomodate the lone piece of "furniture" that sits within. James K. Polk had the room installed in 1846 and called it "my secret water closet." It was later dubbed the "Polk Room."

At the time of its installation, the official Oval Office toilet facilities located off the main hall were being repaired. Polk was a cleanliness nut and had this spare room, originally a broom closet, fitted with a commode and a tiny wash basin.

Once the main bathroom was back on its feet there was no need to use the spare toilet and it sat forgotten for years. Until Rutherford B. Hayes took office in 1877.

His constituents didn't know it but Hayes suffered from (or enjoyed, depending on one's perspective) a condition best described as claustromania, an intense fondness for cramped, closed-in spaces. When the little toilet room off the Oval Office was pointed out to him, he promptly made it his private retreat.

At times of national trouble, when major decisions had to be made, Hayes would withdraw to the Polk Room, lower his drawers, and sit and think.

Without even knowing it, Benjamin Harrison was responsible for the most important physical change to take place in the Polk Room. In late 1889, an African emissary presented the 23rd president with a gift of a toilet seat made of rhinoceros horn. Not knowing what to do with the grotesque gift, Harrison had it installed in the Polk Room, which he never used.

Grover Cleveland, however, had used it during his first hitch as president and, upon reinstatement in 1893, his first desire was to use it again. He was astounded by the extraordinary texture of the new seat. During the first two weeks of his second term in office, only the most pressing business could draw him from his lair.

To Cleveland, the Polk Room was the greatest perquisite of the presidency. When he left office in 1897, weeping silently as the carriage carted him away, newspaper reporters wrote that he grieved at leaving office before his Democratic agenda was completed. In reality, the president bitterly recognized that he'd never get to plant himself on that beloved throne ever again.

In fact, before leaving office he had the wherewithal to issue a secret directive to the next president. Scribbled on a piece of high-grade White House stationery, the note read, "Mr. McKinley: The Polk Room is a presidential privilege. It is my suggestion that you, and you alone, take access to this very special room. I hereby pass on to you the one and only key. G. Cleveland."

William McKinley agreed and he saw to it that all successive presidents would receive a sealed directive outlining recommendations as to the use of the Polk Room.

White House traditions and procedures changed and evolved with the changing times but the rules concerning the Polk Room were written in stone. It was for the president only. Even the most trusted members of the cleaning staff were not allowed within. The presidents themselves took the responsibility of washing it out.

The White House domestic staff witnessed only one brouhaha between Ike and Mamie Eisenhower in all their years there and it involved the use of the Polk Room.

Apparently Ike, in a state of dreamy half-sleep late one night, told Mamie of the wonderful feel of the rhinoceros toilet seat in the Polk Room. Thereafter, whenever she had a chance, she'd pilfer the key from his pants pocket and sneak in there for a quick one.

Ike was furious at finding her there one afternoon when he awoke from his nap earlier than usual. He roared and hollered that HE fought at Normandy, and HE was the president. She was nothing more than first lady, a position that came with the job of being his wife, and she was not entitled to presidential privilege.

On the other hand, LBJ didn't care for the seat and Ladybird did, so there was never an argument when she sat in there for hours on end.

The graffiti on the walls makes interesting reading. "Give 'em hell, Ike!" carries the distinctive scrawl of Harry Truman.

"Nixon did it here!" exemplifies the enigmatic Richard Nixon, who could be bold and brash when no one was watching.

At 10:40 A.M. on January 20, 1993, George Bush moseyed into the Polk Room one last time. At ten to eleven his wife Barbara pounded on the door, pleading with him to hurry so they wouldn't be late for the inauguration of the new president.

At 11:00 sharp, Bill Clinton appeared with military personnel to have the former president dislodged. Breaking the door down, they found Mr.Bush on his hands and knees, frantically trying to remove the seat with a screwdriver.

He wasn't the first to try.

What's Right Is Right

Father Donald Lophenphish sleepily donned his cassock in the sacristy of the church, wondering, as he always did when it was his turn to perform the early mass, why he'd gone into this line of work in the first place. As a young altar boy, he'd hated serving the early mass so much that he questioned his own sanity when he started thinking of the priesthood as a career option at age twenty-eight.

Now the organ droned and a loose flock of devout Catholics awaited his grand entrance. Father Lophenphish yawned as if his life depended on it. He'd stayed up too late last night, drinking gin and playing Trivial Pursuit by himself.

As a priest, Father Don was unique in that he dabbled with magic, hiring himself out to entertain at children's birthday parties and other such events. He prided himself on keeping up with his hobby throughout the grueling years at the seminary and considered himself a top-notch magician.

On this Sunday morning, due to his hangover, or his

tiredness, or the customary combination of both, the inevitable occurred. Father Don mumbled his way through the pages of liturgy, signing the cross, bowing, and genuflecting as if in a trance. As he launched into the offertory prayers, he absentmindedly gave the wrong word and when he lifted his chalice, there appeared a little baby bunny.

Knowing immediately that he'd blathered words from the wrong text, Father Lophenphish panicked and blurted more magic words to make the bunny disappear. His mind and his tongue were on different wavelengths, however, and before he knew it an entire litter of white bunnies were hopping all over the altar.

The congregation stirred and a mild hubbub followed. Old women craned their necks to see what was happening as bunnies leaped to the floor and hopped toward the pews.

Father Don shook his head in an effort to think straight. He uttered a stream of strange words, some English, some Latin, some straight out of his books of magic.

All hell broke loose when dozens of birds fluttered out of his sleeves, dive-bombing the parishioners and taking roost on the rafters high above.

Everyone had to come back for the later mass, grumbling and pissing and moaning. Father Lophenphish took the rest of the day off.

"After all," he said to himself as he unboxed Trivial Pursuit within the quiet confines of his rectory study, "Sunday is supposed to be a day of rest."

The Dog's Life

Margarate O. Cherry sat, elderly, in her overheated living room, listening to old romantic records as the evening wore on relentlessly. Fidgeting and restlessly bristling at each unwelcome outside noise, she tried to relax and remember what these songs had meant to her and dear Robert, her one and only, who three years earlier had been found floating in 30 feet of river water as best one can with weights tied to one's ankles.

"Oh, Robert," Margarate sobbed as an especially memorable verse came through. They were the first words she'd uttered since yesterday afternoon when she'd cursed after slipping on a copy of *Good Housekeeping*, which was lying on the floor with just about everything else.

Despite the fact that in their youth Margarate and Robert had been lovers in the best of ways, the fruit went sour as the years withered on the vine. The last time they saw each other was at the breakfast table on the day of his demise and they were at each other's throats.

But, like the photographs she'd kept of him, the awful memories had turned yellow and the hard edges had faded into soft, pastel yearnings and longings. She'd forgotten his cruelties.

He was a veterinarian and in the early days of their marriage she nagged him incessantly. He administered distemper shots while she was asleep, leaving her lackadaisically lukewarm for days at a time.

Now in her old age, she engaged in behavior that puzzled the neighbors immensely, such as howling from the back porch on moonlit nights, digging holes under the front shrubs with her hands and feet, and chasing milk trucks down the alley when tensions got the best of her. And she'd taken to eating her meals out of bowls on the floor and curling up at night on the rug by the fireplace.

Thank goodness she was wearing her collar the night she wandered out of the neighborhood. Old Walter "Wrinkly" Trinkle, 97 and wrinkled bad, though he'd acquired his nickname when he was just a lad in Denmark, found her and was able to return her to her proper home. They later fell in love and Margarate O. Cherry forgot about What's-His-Name, the veterinarian.

"It's never too late to give up hope," Walter "Wrinkly" Trinkle remarked one night while leading Margarate around on her leash. "I've always wanted a dog but was allergic to the damned things. Now I got you."

And if Margarate had had a tail, it would have been wagging.

The Exploits of Lonnigle Jurré

When Lonnigle Jurré landed a job as manager of the crockery department at Gottslute's Department Store in Omaha, he thought he'd at last arrived. No one who knew of his misery-wracked past could blame him for being excited.

Among other things in his flawed and cheerless life, Lonnigle had valiantly fought off fierce homosexual tendencies, like a shining knight flogging beastly dragons into gelatinous lumps on the rubble of his discontent. He felt he was now over the hump where this was concerned and it would all be downhill from there.

Still haunting him as always, however, were his enlarged breasts, brought on by a mysterious glandular malfunction that puzzled even the most knowledgeable of doctors, such as Dr. William E. Bendanoyve, Lonnigle's family physician, who liked to jiggle them whenever he was given an opportunity.

Highly sensitive about this quirk in his general physique, Lonnigle's ears still burned with the childish taunts to which he was subjected whenever he undressed in the boys' locker room or appeared shirtless at the beach.

"Never mind, Lonnie," his mother would say, turning her nose up at the crude boys as she collared her son and led him to a secluded area of the beach where they could be alone.

By the time he was sixteen his breasts were so large that normal shirts couldn't conceal them. He began wearing thick layers of sweaters and jackets, even in hot weather, which didn't do much for his self-esteem.

Upon graduation from high school, Lonnigle left behind the small town of Earwhip, Nebraska, the nickname "Boobs," and his mother, and headed for the big city, never to return.

Months of psychoanalysis and an unaccountable slight shrinkage of his bustline allowed him to try for gainful employment. The owner of the department store, Melvin Gottslute himself, hired Lonnigle on the spot.

Had Lon (he called himself Lon now, thinking it sounded more manly) known that Mr. Gottslute's motive in hiring him was his wife's flat-chestedness, he'd have been devastated. But the boss only wanted to look, not touch, so Lon was never the wiser.

"You'll do fine," Gottslute said, slapping his new employee on the back to convey encouragement. "Miss Inkblot, your secretary, will be here shortly. Just make yourself comfortable. Customers are starting to arrive. I'll be back later to see how things are going."

"Splendid," Lon said in response.

Lon Jurré strode the aisles amid the glassware, smiling at the browsing customers. He eyed one gentleman who seemed to be looking for something in particular and was about to ask if he could be of assistance, when suddenly his name was announced over the P.A.

"Lon Jurré, line one. Lon Jurré, line one."

Surprised, Lon hurried to the phone on the far wall and punched the button for line one.

"Yes? This is Lon Jurré." The caller might as well have shot him squarely in the forehead with a twelve-gauge shotgun.

"Do you have a size 46 bra?"

Too shocked to even reply, he hung up the phone and stared into space like an idiot, his face red as a beet, his ears burning with a mix of shame and anger.

A customer asked a question but he didn't hear it, fumbling with his tie and mumbling incoherently. Another tried to flag him down as he wandered aimlessly into the stationery department. Again the P.A. called him.

"Lon Jurré, line one. Lon Jurre, line one."

Scrambling back to his desk as quickly as he could, Lon took the call with a hoarse and trembly voice.

"Hello, this is Lon Jurré."

"We must have gotten disconnected," said the caller. "I wanted to know if you've got a size 46 bra."

"No, I don't," Lon said firmly, hanging up and smiling nervously at a woman yelling at her kid not to break anything. "As a matter of fact, I used to wear a size 46," he thought in a panic, "but why should I tell her, a perfect stranger?"

Things quieted down for awhile and Lon was feeling at ease again until another announcement came blaring over the speakers.

"Lon Jurré, line one. Lon Jurré, line one."

Grinning like a fool at the throng of wandering customers, Lon took the phone and, with extreme nervousness, faced the situation as bravely as he could.

"Yes?"

"Hello," spoke the middle-aged dowager. "Do you have a bra in size 52, D cup?"

"No, ma'am, I do not."

"Oh, fudge," she complained. "I've been calling all over. No one seems to have one and a bridge partner of mine suggested I call you. She said she was sure you'd have one."

"No, I'm afraid the person who supplied you with that report has highly exaggerated information."

Again the P.A. blared his name for all to hear.

"Lon Jurré, line two. Lon Jurré, line two."

"Oh, what now?" he asked under his breath. "Hello, Lon Jurré," he said into the receiver as cheerfully as he could under the circumstances. It was a young girl this time.

"Do you have frilly, pink panties?"

"Of course not!" he bellowed, slamming down the phone,

wiping the sweat from his brow.

At four o'clock, Mr. Gottslute appeared at Lon's desk, horrified by the number of customer complaints he'd received concerning poor service in the crockery department.

"What is the meaning of this?" he stormed. "Your receipts on the day are nil! Customers are lined up waiting for service! What in the hell is going on here?"

"The phone has been ringing for me all day," Lon cheeped from behind his desk like an injured bird.

That night Mr. Gottslute went over the accounts carefully. Lon Jurré had been fired. His poor performance was responsible for the dismal sales in crockery.

But why, *why* were sales down in the lingerie department?

Bladder Gone Snafu

Rolf Stebbins entered Hillcrest Memorial Hospital on June 10, 1994, with a bladder gone snafu. He needed an operation but bad.

"Would you like anesthesia A, anesthesia B, or good old brand X?" offered Dr. Malcolm Groap.

"What does the public prefer?" Rolf Stebbins asked.

The answer was...not what happened to him. He died on the operating table.

Rolf Stebbins hadn't been rich but years earlier he'd prepaid his funeral expenses and was now reaping the rewards. The casket, the embalming of the body, the church services, even the sloppy-joe dinner in the church basement for those attending the funeral, were all taken care of.

However, his family, which consisted of one irresponsible nephew named Ralph Nedgewick, was informed by those in charge of such things that transportation of the body was not covered. This was a thorn in the skin of Ralph

Nedgewick since Rolf Stebbins died while on vacation in Las Vegas and was to be buried in his hometown of Bean Blossom, Indiana.

Ralph Nedgewick grudgingly boarded a DC-10 out of Indianapolis in order to positively identify his uncle in the Las Vegas morgue, as transportation of an unidentified stiff is against federal law.

Imagine Ralph's dismay when he was told upon his return to Bean Blossom that his uncle's body had been lost in the shuffle at the Denver airport and left behind.

"They can send it on with the next available flight, can't they?" he barked into the phone. "Aaarrrrrrggggg!" he screamed across the wires when he was informed that there were two other unclaimed caskets at the baggage area and that they had somehow gotten mixed up. He'd have to come to Denver to make another positive identification.

"The hell with it," he said, filled with utter disgust. He packed all his things and moved to Denver to avoid having to make another return flight. Rolf Stebbins was buried without fanfare in a churchyard on the outskirts of Denver.

There was no sloppy-joe dinner, which greatly disappointed Clara Squeegee, long-time family acquaintance, who was planning to make that her social event of the month.

Could Something Be Dreadfully Wrong?

Mrs. O. Michael O'Paddywagon lay in bed reading *Plush* magazine. She sighed quietly and pulled the satin higher, covering her shapeless breasts.

She heard her husband's footsteps out in the hall. He'd been downstairs watching television, or reading, or using the telephone to conduct late-night business with clients.

He entered the bedroom without a word, took off his

clothes, and walked into the adjoining bathroom. Mrs. O'Paddywagon put her magazine down and, closing her eyes, listened.

The water flowed into the sink for fifteen seconds, then was abruptly turned off. She heard her husband gargle like a drowning frog, then there was silence.

"Three, two, one," she counted in her mind, and the water rushed into the sink again, this time for twenty seconds before it was turned off with a thud.

There was a click and a quiet clatter, followed by the sound of her husband brushing his teeth. He spit, and the water ran again.

He turned it off, spit again, and tapped his toothbrush against the side of the washbasin once…twice…

Mrs. O. Michael O'Paddywagon leaped from her bed, flowing silk nightie and all. Her heart in her throat, she hammered on the door.

"Noodlemunchkins, are you all right?"

Mr. O'Paddywagon swung the door open wide. Staring straight ahead, he brushed her aside as if she were a piece of lint on his lapel.

"I felt like tapping my toothbrush only twice tonight," he said, sinking into bed. Feeling slightly foolish, Mrs. O. Michael O'Paddywagon settled in next to her husband.

She had trouble sleeping that night, worried that her husband was losing his consistency, which she'd always seen as his best quality. By morning, however, she was overrun with quivers of excitement.

"Maybe there's hope for some zest in this marriage yet," she said as she dusted the fine furniture in the foyer.

The Dance of the Flamingos

Sybil Slappem, young, ambitious elementary school

teacher, had one utterly obnoxious habit: correcting people's use of the English language.

She'd ruined her younger siblings' childhood by castigating them until they ranted and raved, even in their sleep. After they finally moved out, Sybil went into teaching, where she felt she'd be free to pester students mercilessly about keeping straight their p's and q's.

This wasn't enough for her, however. Sybil, by virtue of her radar ears, caught store clerks and parking attendants, street sweepers and insurance agents, traffic cops and museum guides with their grammatical pants down and never hesitated to let them have it.

She turned it into a one woman crusade, penciling in corrections on misworded signs and leaving short language lessons on telephone answering machines. But she met her match one day while stalking the city sidewalks in search of indiscretions in verbiage.

"Flamingo Dancing Lessons on Second Floor," the sign read. Sybil blew a gasket.

She stormed up the stairs, blew open the door, and roared, "May I speak to the *flamenco* dance instructor, please?"

"There ain't one here," came the reply from a tall, dark, handsome man who waltzed around the dimly lit room with his arms cradling a spindle-legged pink flamingo.

His name was Don Cornelius Ploszynski and Sybil fell in love with him on the spot. She quit her job and began working with him, teaching flamingos to dance.

"I ain't never had so much fun," he gurgled, brushing against his wife as they pirouetted their flamingos at the same time in the center of the dance floor.

"Me neither," she said, and there was no argument.

A Day in the Life at Permashrink

Raylene Dolinda Guantanamo enjoyed working with hair, shampooing it, combing it, cutting it. But one day it dawned on her that there was one thing about being a hairdresser she just couldn't stand anymore: the gabbing.

"What the hell am I going to talk about today with those bags and biddies at the shop?" she wondered. Because of the need to make small talk, she began to dread having to go to work at all.

This was a dire strait for a hairdresser. She'd exhausted her supply of small talk and chitchat and she was only twenty-six.

"Today I have Mrs. Habishem on my schedule," she groaned. "That fat hog. And tomorrow Joyce Riffkiller, bad breath, oily hair condition and all."

Raylene did the only thing she could do under these circumstances. She called in sick.

After much soul-searching and agonizing, Raylene hit upon an idea that was certain to resurrect her career. It was a stroke of genius, the inspiration of a lifetime.

She quit her job and enrolled in courses at the state university. Six years later she graduated with a degree in clinical psychology. It had been rough at times, making ends meet. To put meals on the table, Raylene worked the third shift as a podiatrist's assistant at an around-the-clock foot clinic. But it had been worth it.

On July 1, 1991, Permashrink, Inc. opened its doors. Raylene had never been prouder. She beamed as her mother photographed her in front of the shop, the sign above in yellow lights for all the world to see:

PERMASHRINK, INC.
Total Head Treatment
"Beauty Inside and Out"
Raylene Dolinda Guantanamo, owner

She'd come a long way since her early days at Betty's Beauty Barn, that was for sure.

So now, instead of gabbing endlessly about nothing in general, Raylene Dolinda Guantanamo sudses and clips her customers' hair while they go on and on about how their fathers had tormented them and how their mothers still won't leave them alone.

"Hmm-mm, what else happened when you were six?" she prompts as she goops on the Hi-Protein Hair Permanent Putty. Her business cards read, "Raylene Dolinda Guantanamo, Full Treatment, Inside and Out."

She doesn't wake up in the morning frantically thinking of interesting tidbits anymore. She merely has to convince herself that she cares about the childhood trials and traumas of the bags and biddies who wander into Permashrink, Inc.

The Perils of Ringo Santana

Ringo Santana lived a charmed life. Opportunities and outright miracles had a way of dropping plumb into his lap, whether he wanted them to or not.

Born and reared in a small Midwestern town, Ringo became one of the most sought-after football prospects in the nation. His parents, hard-working owners of a small produce stand, were totally unable to grasp what was happening to their son when the recruiters swarmed on him in the summer of '75.

Southern Cal won him over and after an illustrious career there as a record-breaking tailback, he went on to play for the Miami Dolphins, where he became a playboy jock of international proportions.

While at the height of his football career, he made guest appearances on prime-time TV shows, leading to Academy Award-winning roles in major motion pictures.

An album of sentimental ballads paved the way to another lucrative career as a touring rock singer. His promoters had his face on posters, pencil boxes, and pillow cases. His name was even bandied about by the Republican Party in Florida as a possible candidate for the Senate.

But, as with all celebrities whose lives are too good to be true, Ringo Santana's life was a mess.

After a sell-out crowd of teenie-boppers nearly tore him apart during his third encore, Ringo poured his heart out to his manager, Glinda Woszniak. He told her he'd had enough.

"I always wanted to go into insurance," he said and she saw a light in his eyes that she had never seen before. With growing enthusiasm he explained that his feelings could no longer be denied.

"I never should have listened to those recruiters back in high school," he stated passionately. "I knew then what I really wanted and I've wasted all these years."

Being an insurance salesman had always been Ringo's secret goal. A nun had praised the neatness of his work when he was in third grade and he'd loved doing worksheets ever since. Filling out insurance forms, he figured, was the closest he could come to doing worksheets for a living.

"The terminology is fascinating," he gushed. "Premiums, limits of liability, coverage exclusions, renewal discounts. The list is endless." Glinda Woszniak felt sick to her stomach.

Ringo Santana didn't do well in insurance. Too late, he tried to revive his singing career but his time was past.

He sang and played acoustic guitar in run-down restaurants and clubs until even they didn't want him. The last he played was at the grand opening of a pet shop, where the customers grew annoyed with his singing because they couldn't hear what the clerk was saying about the tropical fish.

Ringo quit working entirely and sponged off his old friend Portly Entwhistle Cheesecake, world famous rotund male model. Entwhistle was so frequently described with the word 'portly' in newspaper gossip columns that in 1985 he had his name legally changed to include it on a permanent basis.

A Match Made Somewhere Between Heaven and Hell

E. Worthington Phillipshead, who had money even in his underwear, felt adventurous one spring afternoon and went for a small stroll without his usual cortege.

He snuck out the back with his valet, Albert, his young ward, Dudley, and his Aunt Rosetta's stepson, Charley, who was visiting from either Oregon or Georgia, as he had two homes.

The annual Phillipshead Estate Backgammon Tournament was under way, and E. Worthington's staff of consultants, advisors, and bodyguards were absorbed in their games, with their heads down, so it was easy to get away unnoticed.

It wasn't often that E. Worthington Phillipshead found himself in such a position. Being one of the richest men on earth and the major mover and shaker of business affairs on the east coast, he rarely felt comfortable in public, afraid of recognition and its unpleasant results.

But today, however, he felt different. He was sick of seeing the same stuffed shirts and answering the same telephones. Young again, he walked and chatted freely with his companions, breathing in the fresh air and taking in the sights.

E. Worthington led the way, and promptly they were lost. His sense of direction had never been good but he relied on it anyway and despite arguments from the others, he took them farther and farther from the estate in an effort to find his way back.

In truth, he was having the time of his life. Oblivious to the fact that he was leading them into seedier surroundings with each step, he talked on and on. The latest fashion oddities from Paris, his friends' near-disastrous plane ride back from Japan, the new items on the menu at his favorite Broadway restaurant, any topic was fair game as long as it had nothing to do with the drudgery of work.

They passed a burned out storefront and a dingy dilapidated hotel. Broken glass crunched under their feet and bad smells emanated from between buildings. A frazzled, worn-out man slept on the steps of a boarded-up jewelry store. They encountered three drunk men arguing incoherently in an alley.

E. Worthington's companions were becoming agitated. E. Worthington himself didn't seem to notice his immediate environment. He babbled on, now about the baseball card collection of his boyhood, then about his favorite vacation spots in Mexico.

They rounded a corner where a society-forsaken gentleman sorted garbage in a trashbin and made their way toward the riverfront. They walked over the rubble of an abandoned mill, on to a row of warehouses. There was no life on the street, the river was stagnant with odiferous sludge, litter was strewn far and wide.

Just when E. Worthington veered off in the right direction and his companions began to breathe easier, a momentous event unfolded.

There, in a crevice between buildings, stood a woman who looked like yesterday's newspaper left out in the rain. Her gray, scraggly hair hung down in greasy bunches and ragged sweatshirts wrapped her bent frame. With tattered longjohns bunching up at her ankles, she shuffled her feet in a pair of unmatched men's shoes.

Her hands were chapped and gnarled, her face scarred and splotched with red. Teeth were missing.

At her side was a bag containing her worldly possessions: two dirty, worn-out sweatshirts, a mass of folded tissue paper, a plastic storage container with wooden disks inside, twelve scarves, a wallet filled with old newspaper clippings, and a few other pieces of assorted flotsam.

E. Worthington Phillipshead was in mid-sentence when he saw her standing there. His words might as well have been chopped by an angry ax. She looked at him and their eyes were magnets, drawing them together.

They embraced on the crumbling sidewalk, passionately kissing, their mouths open and wet. E. Worthington's retinue stood dumbfounded. The two hugged and kissed for a full three minutes before either said a word.

Her name was Revlon Slick, and to E. Worthington she was a goddess. Talking and laughing all the way back to the estate, it seemed they'd known each other all their lives.

"If I'd known I would meet you, I'd have fixed myself up a bit," she said.

"Never mind," E. Worthington slobbered. "I can't wait to take you to the upcoming state convention of the Republican Party."

But things didn't work out. Revlon Slick didn't want to leave her world behind for his and the feeling was mutual where he was concerned. They had an amicable parting, which included a magnificent gala on the grounds of the estate.

Friends from both sides received invitations. For the first times in their lives, the street people attending were eating caviar and drinking champagne. The rich playboys tried flat muscatel imported from Spain in dirty, half-filled bottles and smoked soggy cigar butts compiled by Phillipshead servants from the city gutters.

A grand time was had by all.

"My Ass Stinks"

Barrington Colby sat drinking concoctions, gazing out at

the Illinois skyline, waiting for a midnight sun.

"I don't mind going to work," he muttered to no one. "It's arriving that I hate."

His radio shook static news from the prickly airwaves: "A police spokesman said vain attempts will be made to track the killer."

Long ago Barrington Colby had unpacked his mind, knowing it wasn't going anywhere. He put it in his back pocket and flattened it as he sat while others traveled.

"The jury declared themselves insane..." the radio droned in fits of distant static.

"I don't clean my toilet bowl," Barrington announced to himself. "It reminds me of where I've been and where I'm going." He trembled involuntarily.

"...remains in critical condition. The other victim, who suffered a gunshot wound to the instep, is in fantastic condition, owing to the fact that he's surrounded by scantily clan young vixens who are trying to see if they can wangle any money out of him."

"My ass stinks," Barrington moaned with acute realization.

"...with a blood-alcohol level of.225%. By Illinois law,.1% is considered drunk as a skunk."

"I'm tired of my conscience gnawing away at me like a termite at the core of my brain," Barrington Colby complained.

"...and the president is sending in troops to restore the calm..."

"It's your world," he sighed, addressing no one in particular. "I'm just living in it."

"We'll return to our program of uninterrupted easy listening music after this word from our sponsor..."

"I'm sick of looking forward to my lousy future," Barrington Colby grieved like an open wound on the face of humanity.

The Noisemaker-Maker

Russ Crimbley, maker of noisemakers, had been staying up late at the shop trying to fill orders. With New Year's fast approaching, he was up to his waist in work.

Kazoos, tin trumpets, rattles, and wooden ratchets were his specialties. He'd been perfecting his craft for over sixty years.

One night at the height of the season, he trudged home, sipped a quiet mug of hot tea, and tucked himself into bed. His weary eyes closed the world out and his thoughts floated down like fluffy feathers slowly sinking into a bed of cotton clouds. Then he heard it.

It started with a series of inconsistent clicks, like a geiger counter's first brush with a hidden radioactive substance. It persisted and rattled Russ right out of his bed.

It was Lucretia Golldang, middle-aged divorcee from across the hall, practicing her castanets again. Russ calmly plodded to her door and knocked.

When she answered the door, he blew her across the room with an elephant gun.

"Nuff said," said he.

The Bother of Our Country

"You'd stand up in boats as well, if you had boils the size of mine on your ass," George Washington said to his wife, Martha, who wouldn't stop criticizing her husband for his indiscretion.

"But, George, think of the children," she persisted. "They see you doing it, they'll want to do it themselves."

"So be it," the broken man said, old beyond his years.

Martha bustled off to bake her daily whiskey-cake, disgusted with her husband all over again. For being such a brave and noble warrior, George was an unhealthy cuss, besieged at all times by chronic maladies and discomforts, none debilitating but nevertheless annoying for those within earshot.

"Always huffing and puffing, moaning and groaning, squeaking and creaking," Martha muttered, taking a swig for good measure.

It was true about George. The first president of the United States was nothing but a complainer.

Hangnails, corns, irregular heartbeat, swollen joints, lumbago. Food allergies, headaches, a trick knee, buzzing in the ears, poorly fitting false teeth, gout. Rashes and goiters, gall stones and fevers, itchy scalp and indigestion, low blood sugar and more.

Worst of all were the boils on his posterior, rising then falling, festering then relenting, but never leaving him completely alone.

They're the reason Gilbert Stewart was unable to finish his portrait. A guy can pose standing stark-still for only so long before his legs turn to jelly or fall into a tingling sleep. And due to the horrific boils, George's options were reduced to standing or lying on his stomach, the latter not conducive to getting a portrait painted.

The boils were the ultimate plague of his life. They're the reason for the grim and somber countenance that graces our one dollar bills and every other likeness we have of him today. They also led to out-and-out havoc in his personal life.

Dr. Hiram O'Geezer, upon learning of the stubborn boils, recommended a strict diet of nothing but carrot juice. Within a week George's skin was yellow-orange.

Martha couldn't bear to look at him. Her father, who used to beat her with hickory switches for no good reason, had suffered from yellow jaundice most of his adult life. One look at George's tinted face opened a flood of gruesome memories that overcame her with such clarity that she was forced to flee to the nearby woods.

Martha's sense of direction was her weakest link and she

was lost out there for days, until a neighbor, Horace Mennorpile, finally responded to her screams. He helped her down from a tree where wolves had chased her.

Horace Mennorpile wasn't any happier when he learned it was the fault of George's continuing problems with his boils. "He's the bother of our country," he mumbled as he trudged across the Virginia fields, returning to his own life and his own batch of troubles.

Releasing the Bulge

A red light held the traffic for ransom at the corner of Beasley and Crow. Martha Squird was startled from her musings by the frantic waving of the man in the car in the next lane. She rolled her window down to see what he wanted.

"My pants are too tight!" the balding, red-faced man bellowed. His state of agitation was clear. Sweat ran from his jowls, veins flexed in his neck, his face winced with contortions of pain. His eyes bugged out at poor Martha, filling her with alarm.

"Loosen your belt!" she screamed as her car roared off into the city tangle.

Indeed, Axlerod Freengoggle's belt had been too tight. Once he loosened it as directed, he was able to breathe again, at least temporarily. Prompted by an impatient driver's loud honk, he sighed and drove on to work.

Once in his office, Axlerod began to fidget and squirm again. His pants were tight like never before and he couldn't find relief. It was then that he realized with horror that he was the proverbial "expanding bulge in a three-piece suit" his mother had always talked about.

He had to interrupt his first phone client due to extreme discomfort. "I don't think I can finish the call," he gasped.

"What seems to be the trouble?" asked the executive on

the other end.

"My belt is...incredibly tight," Axlerod explained. "I think I might have to go home."

"Just loosen your belt," the man suggested. Annoyed for not thinking of this himself, Axlerod was pleased to find that loosening his belt indeed brought relief. They finished their business and the blob signed off with thanks.

"But there's only so many notches in the ordinary belt," he quipped with a nervous laugh.

At the big board meeting an hour later, Axlerod Freengoggle had a hard time concentrating on what Mr. Tytnutz was blathering about, due to his expanding condition that wouldn't relent for anything.

He tried everything to get his mind off his troubles: counting sheep, holding his breath, rolling his eyeballs back in their sockets as far as they would go. Nothing worked.

At last he dashed off a note and passed it to the head of the table. Mr. Tytnutz read it solemnly.

"The next item on our agenda is Mr. Freengoggle's condition. The note here says his pants are too tight. It's my position that it would be well worth a try to loosen said pants, if by no other means than by easing the belt into a new position."

"Hear, hear, J.B.!" the others chorused in agreement. Axlerod yanked on the leather belt and slipped the tab on the buckle into the next hole, effectively loosening the belt and relieving himself of the strangle-hold.

The phone was ringing as he reentered his office after the meeting. It was his girlfriend, Laura Bottombunk III.

"Hello, Axlerod," she whined sweetly through her nose. "I'm just calling to tell you that I'm not going to be able to meet you tonight after all. I have to get my hair done and I'm having my face recaulked."

"Aw, that's too bad, honey," he said sadly. "Are you having a total overhaul or just a minor tuckpointing?" Before Laura could answer, Axlerod dropped the phone, doubling over in pain. Like the ground shifting in an earthquake, his flesh quaked and spasmed and bulged even more.

An ambulance was called. The rescue worker immediately loosened Axlerod's belt and not a moment too soon.

That afternoon Axlerod Freengoggle joined a nudist colony in a neighboring state, leaving his high-pressure job and nagging girlfriend behind.

"Finally, a position with room for expansion," he muttered as he lay on the beach, letting it all hang out. "It doesn't pay much but so what?" he said as seagulls squawked overhead.

Presently he met Yolanda Schnibble and the two fell in love despite their flabby bodies, sagging asses and all. Yolanda was a down-on-her-luck inventor and unsuccessful entrepreneur. Hers could have been a household name if the breaks and bounces of life hadn't bounced her into the ditch of despair time after time after time.

Being independently wealthy, her failures in the drawing room didn't make much of a difference to anyone other than she herself and her ego, which was scarred beyond recognition anyway.

She thought she'd hit it big at age 34 when she patented "Lazy Specs," a pair of glasses with periscope lenses that allowed a person lying on a couch to watch TV without lifting their head from the sofa pillow.

"Take the fatigue out of TV watching with 'Lazy Specs!'" the ads screamed. But much to Yolanda's surprise, even people who watch too much TV have some self-respect. They didn't sell.

She toiled away with an electronic approach next, devoting ten years to the development of "The Penis Ring" and "The Smoker's Watch."

"The Penis Ring" was a battery-powered metal ring that slipped over a man's flaccid penis, wired to pick up stimuli (body heat, heart rate, testosterone levels, various other factors) to alert the man that urination was necessary.

Small electronic jolts were delivered to the penis to remind the user to make his way to the nearest restroom to find alleviation. At first the jolts were infrequent and of low intensity but the longer the wait and the greater the urgency, the stronger and more regular were the electric shocks.

"The Penis Ring" never took off and was yanked from the market when lawsuits arose as a result of several cases of neural damage caused by the rings being worn during unexpected erection.

Yolanda Schnibble's other invention of this era was "The Smoker's Watch," an ingenious piece of work. An ordinary wristwatch rigged with an alarm, The Smoker's Watch could be set at regular intervals to remind the user that it was time for a cigarette. Once again small electric shocks zapped the user, this time in the flesh of the wrist.

For a light smoker, it was suggested that the watch be set for thirty to forty minutes. Heavy chain smokers would have to adjust the dial on the side to activate the electric pulses every three or four minutes or so.

It never caught on.

Ms. Schnibble gained a modicum of success and respect with her last idea, which wasn't really an invention at all. She came up with a line of colorful lapel buttons that allowed the users to announce their latest triumphs to the world at large.

"New and Improved!" they crowed, meaning the wearer had recently changed in a positive way. Passersby were to scan the fine print below to learn what it was that made the wearer "new" and "improved."

New and Improved!
Hasn't nagged husband
for over a week.

New and Improved!
Stopped drinking
charcoal lighter fluid.

New and Improved!
Lost 40 pounds
since January.

New and Improved!
Am taking a class
at the university.

New and Improved!
Stopped leaving crumbs
on the table
in the lounge at work.

New and Improved!
Stopped bothering
old girlfriend
for dumping me
like a wet fish.

New and Improved!
Haven't had erection trouble
in a helluva long time.

New and Improved!
No longer hides small items
that belong to wife
just to irritate her.

Only Yolanda Schnibble would come up with such an engaging idea as these positive message lapel buttons and try to sell them in a nudist colony.

The Life of a Wife of a Doctor

"I never thought I'd be the wife of a doctor," Cornelia Carbunkle cried as she danced between and around the housework strewn all over the place.

"Then again," she added as she dusted a sculpture of her hubby's grandfather, "I never thought much about nothing at all."

And That Was That

Olaf Oldenberger-Barnwreck and his wife, Pat, flitted about the apartment like a couple of moths at a streetlight, primping the flowers and straightening the chairs. Their guests would be arriving in an hour and the food was festering on the stove.

"Oh no!" cried Pat, crestfallen like a sand castle doused

by an angry wave. "There's a hole in our good tablecloth!"

"What?" sputtered Olaf, coming to see for himself, although he fully believed his wife. "How did that happen?"

"I don't know," she bleated. "Just help me remove it before the guests arrive." The place settings that had been carefully constructed earlier were now dismantled and the bare wood of the table was exposed, nicks, discolorations, and all.

This was just the beginning of their social cave-in. The pudding burned and the dog shit on the rug. A pipe burst and the meat overcooked. The milk was sour and a grease fire filled the house with reeking smoke. The microwave turned the corn to rubber and the dog shit on the rug again.

"Call the guests and cancel the gathering," Pat moaned. "Tell them something's come up and we'll do it again some other time."

After Olaf returned from the task, he sat and wondered, "What are we going to do with all this food and everything?"

"Seems a shame to let it go to a complete waste," Pat said. Olaf slogged his way to the phone again. He sat in the chair like a ton of bricks being dropped from a small height and began dialing.

"Who are you calling?" asked Pat.

"People we hate who we owe a dinner," Olaf said, and that's what he did and that was that.

Another Argument

Weeby Floynpoop sat watching TV. His wife, Fannie, chased their children from one side of the house to the other.

"Weeb!" she cried. "You've got to do something about these damned kids!"

"What can I do about 'em?" he asked, annoyed at missing the introductory remarks of a new show he'd been waiting five minutes to see.

"I want you to get a vasectomy, that's what!" she bellowed, trying to snatch the eight-year-old as he swung past on the chandelier.

"I ain't getting no vasectomy," he said, kicking the baby out of his line of vision. "No doctor's gonna cut off *my* balls."

"They don't cut off your balls," she said as dishes rained down from the china hutch. "They snip your vas deferens."

"I'll say there'd be a vast difference," he mumbled, his heavy thumb planted firmly on the volume button of the remote.

Raunch Twiddley, Trusty Plumber

"Fancy neighborhood," Raunch Twiddley commented to himself as he scanned addresses, trying to spy 2106 Concrete Meadow Trail. He found it and, with the butterflies in the stomach that always accompanied him when he was about to begin work on an unfamiliar set of pipes, he lugged his equipment up the winding walk to the door.

A bored maid let him in, he handed her his "Raunch Twiddley—Have Pipe Wrench, Will Travel" calling card, and she pointed to the troublespot: the guts of the kitchen sink. Raunch knew his stuff and soon had the pipes dismantled and thrown into a tangle on the floor.

"It's a dirty shame," he muttered. "Clogged and corroded through and through. You'd think people would have more respect for their pipes than to continually run water through them without even a thought as to how the insides are rusting and glutting with solidified sludge. It's just a crying shame."

Without warning, Raunch twisted a pipe that broke off in the teeth of his wrench. Water shot up and splattered the ceiling with the force of a small-to-medium-sized cannon.

The maid didn't think twice before calling for emergency

assistance as Raunch Twiddley wrestled frantically with the spouting pipe. In minutes the entire first floor was flooded. The damage estimates were heavy.

That night Raunch Twiddley sat relaxing with his loving family when he suffered a massive heart attack. Rushed like mad to the hospital, he was greeted by Dr. Theobald "Third Degree" Burns, whose house Raunch had trashed earlier that day.

As it turned out, Raunch's pipes were rather clogged themselves and heavy-duty coronary reconstruction had to be performed. Raunch lay recuperating a short while later, no worse for wear.

The family couldn't thank the doctor enough but when they did he gladly accepted. In fact, he charmed them with funny remarks and medical puns on into the night.

So enamored were they with his witticisms, they, as a group, moved in with him and his wife the following weekend, leaving Raunch Twiddley alone and disillusioned.

The Bermuda Triangle

It was the day before school let out for the summer in Hamilton, Bermuda, and the fourth graders in Room 109 were running wild, shouting and screaming and jumping off desktops. Their teacher, Miss Olivia Crink, couldn't hear herself think. But Billy Olson, clairvoyant in the back row, could.

In fact, he was getting quite an education concerning his teacher's sexual fantasies. He'd never seen the janitor, Mr. Broomsmith, as the virile sort, but apparently his teacher did.

That night, as Mr. Broomsmith swept the last of the broken bones and bloody chins under the exit door mat, Miss Crink sat alone at home, crying.

"When I first saw him with his broom," she bawled to her

cat, Liversausage, "I thought he'd sweep me off my feet someday. Instead, he mopped me into a corner and left me there, alone and afraid to move, lest I muddy his nice, clean floor."

Mr. Broomsmith, exhausted at midnight, collapsed into bed, thinking about Marilyn Monroe.

Billy Olsen, lying awake in his bed across town, wondered why.

How the Harwoods Ruined Christmas Forever for Everyone

It all began when John Harwood, father of four, fell behind in his work and his Christmas shopping in December of 1996. Something had to give.

His wife, Veronda, put up a fuss at first, but there was little she could do. John would be out of town on business over the holidays and the only workable solution was to celebrate Christmas later.

The following year John was out of a job entirely but nonetheless fell behind again in preparing for the holidays. Once again the Harwood family observed the festivities in early January instead of at the customary time.

Veronda, surprisingly, was the one to suggest they make a habit of it thereafter, proclaiming January 10th as their personal Christmas Day. The advantages were many.

While everyone else ran around in madness in the middle of December, the Harwoods relaxed and enjoyed each other's company. They shopped after the Christmas rush when the stores were empty and the prices down.

They decorated the house with items purchased cheap at after-Christmas sales. The family cruised the back alleys on January 5th or so for the best discarded Christmas tree available. If they were lucky they'd find one already tinseled and even if not, it was free.

Relatives dropped by unexpectedly at the wrong time one year and discovered the sneaky business. Word got out and most of the people in their North Dakota neck of the woods agreed it made sense to celebrate Christmas the Harwoods' way.

The next Christmas, merchants noticed a distinct decline in profits. Shelves of Christmas decorations gathered dust and unsold Christmas trees cluttered street corners.

The year after that, just as many carolers could be heard ten days after Christmas as ten days before. Christmas in the Harwoods' tradition spread to Minnesota, Wisconsin, Illinois and beyond. At last the president of the United States had to step in.

"I declare December 25th the official day of celebration for Christmas," he blabbed into the mike on national TV. "Anyone caught celebrating it on any other date will be drawn and quartered by our own U.S. Marines."

But, for all his bluster and blather, no one listened to him, and it was virtually impossible to enforce the new law anyway.

Once it caught on, no one celebrated Christmas on the old date anymore; no one wanted to pave the way for others to have a cheap and carefree holiday season.

But with everyone celebrating it on January 10th, the same old problems cropped up again. When a sizable number of citizens chose January 20th as the day of observance to avoid the tangle, things were totally out of hand.

It wasn't long before everyone, other than a few religious fanatics, quit celebrating Christmas altogether.

Another Storm in the Forecast

It was bad enough when Sonny Storm's son, Sherman,

returned from his latest concert tour with a padlock punkishly embedded in his cheek. But when the boy announced that he'd dubbed his band "The Fallen Barometers," as he'd been threatening to for weeks, Sonny, being a TV meteorologist, knew there were storm clouds ahead.

"This, in my eyes, is an out-and-out affront on the respectability I've been garnering little by little for ages on end!" screamed the father.

Famous throughout the Boston viewing area for his bland TV forecasts and absolute inability to distinguish "mostly sunny" from "partly cloudy," Sonny Storm knew his son's stab in the groin would make the gossip columns and the rounds of office patter he so diligently tried to avoid.

It's not easy walking the tightrope between anonymity and fame. He wanted his ratings to be passable, of course, but he didn't want people prying into his affairs and digging into his dirt.

The skeleton that especially haunted him was the debacle in Seattle when, without the station manager's permission, he went ahead and authorized payment of $20,000 to a local artist to sculpt several ice statues for the station's winter festival. He was promptly fired and laughed out of town when his forecast went awry and balmy weather moved in, melting the grandiose sculptures before more than a handful of people could view them.

Now his own flesh and blood loomed on the horizon like a menacing gale of humiliation just waiting to happen. And there wasn't much he could do. Sonny had already disowned his son more times than he could remember, but it never did any good. Sherman always came back.

Sonny's wife, Maybelle, was too kind-hearted to see her son banished outright. She made it clear that he would always be welcome back home, much to her seething husband's displeasure.

The struggle finally came to a head when Sonny died after being struck by a car outside the TV station. He'd hypnotized himself staring into the Doppler radar machine and wandered out into traffic.

"At Last the Storm is Over," his tombstone read.

Entertaining the Old Birds

Frisco Butternoodle knew what he liked and he hated himself very much. Headache and all, he walked through the park one summer's day. It was hard to believe he'd ever been a cute little baby, so gray, bloated, and splotchy-skinned was he.

Sitting on a park bench, Frisco deftly rolled a cigarette, then stashed it in the pocket of his worn and ragged sport coat for later.

He watched with interest as a flock of pigeons gathered at the far side of the clearing. They poked and pecked, looking for tidbits in the grass.

A brisk wind pulled at their feathers and made Frisco Butternoodle clutch his sport coat tighter. He got up from the bench and, lowering his head, walked into the wind and over to the birds.

As he approached, more than half flew away. The old birds, who knew from experience that an elderly man in a city park is no great threat, remained. They paced and pecked, keeping a steady eye on the stranger.

Frisco Butternoodle got within twenty feet of the old birds before he stopped and stared at them without emotion. He reached into his pocket and pulled out three balls.

With his eyebrows arching and bending in time with his hands, he juggled with surprising proficiency. The birds stopped what they were doing, training their eyes on the moving spheres. Some grew bored eventually and resumed their search for seeds and crumbs.

Next, Frisco dropped to his hands and knees and, with

effort, turned himself upside down, knees and elbows bent, looking like a scarecrow blown upside down in the wind. With shaking muscles, he straightened his arms and legs and stood stiff and tall, feet high in the air, blood rushing to his head.

After tumbling to the grass, he sat thinking for a moment. The birds moved a trifle farther away and cast looks of suspicion now.

With a hint of excitement, Frisco took a quarter from his pocket and performed a disappearing coin trick for the old birds. In response they jabbed at the grass with their hungry beaks and worked their wings back and forth with nervousness.

Frisco did a soft-shoe in the grass, humming "Look at Me I'm Wonderful." The birds did their best to politely ignore him.

Unbeknownst to Frisco, a middle-aged couple had been watching his performance from a picnic area partially obscured by the brush. Curious, they strolled over to see what this was all about, interrupting a knot-tying demonstration.

Frisco cut the trick short, quickly gathered his scattered materials, and turned to depart.

"Well, *somebody's* got to do it," he said with a shrug. Then he walked away.

Memoirs of a Sanitation Engineer

"Damn," Harvey Verminmingler moaned, on the edge of his seat with pen poised. For the umpteenth time, he'd rushed to his desk with something to add to his memoirs, but by the time he got there he forgot what he was going to write. "I'll never get my cookies finished at this rate."

He read over the beginning of his manuscript. "It was the best of jobs, it was the worst of jobs." That's as far as he'd gotten since he'd decided to write his autobiography, to be titled: *Memoirs of a Garbage Man in Small Town America.*

Harvey trudged back to the kitchen, where he was in the middle of simultaneously kneading cookie dough and cleaning his filthy nails, which got pretty bad in the course of a week on his job. Since discovering the cookie-making method of cleaning his nails several months ago, he'd gained weight that caused his stomach to overflow his belt like thick, gelatinous sludge expanding out of a cylindrical bowl. His wife, Clarice, a cleanliness nut, insisted on the weekly cleanings.

As time slid into the future like a blot of grease melting down the side of a hot oven, Harvey periodically added to his memoirs. But it all came to naught when he died in his sleep one cold autumn night. After the funeral and the resulting hubbub, his wife tossed the papers into the trash.

A garbage picker by the name of Sam Dredges discovered them on a steamy cold Saturday morning and recognized them as a true work of art, as only a person so acquainted with garbage would.

Sam Dredges was a self-proclaimed "backyard-armchair philosopher, psychologist, and dental hygienist" (forever pestering others to floss).

Sam was fond of expounding on his favorite topic: that his job of garbage picker and treasure finder was the calling of a lifetime, more desirable than any two jobs anyone else could name, and he had the feeble arguments to prove it. He once sat on a threadbare, three-legged sofa out by the back alley, instructing a group of children who found themselves taking him seriously.

"What could be better than what I do?" he asked with infectious enthusiasm. "First, there's your fresh air and sunshine. Second, you get your exercise in every day. Three, you find valuables, *if* you know where to look and what to look for. It's an art and it don't come easy.

"Four, you lighten the burden on the landfills. Five, you

got a chance for advancement. At any time you can chuck it and go into something more respectable."

He never got to number six, which had to do with having no union dues to pay. A garbage truck rumbled up the alley, coming to a screeching halt right at Sam's feet.

"Is this a pick-up or a delivery?" asked the driver of the truck.

"You tell me," Sam replied. Minutes later, the truck drove off, heavier in some respects, lighter in others.

"What's the difference anyway?" Sam asked, but by now the kids had found greener pastures in the farm fields across the way.

What to Do About Nothing

Eileen Allittle, faithful chiropractor of Glenwood Falls, sat in the kitchen dreading the return of her husband from work. It was getting to be a habit.

She'd grown tired of his namby-pamby ways. Each morning she had to appraise his attire, going to great lengths to convince him that he looked presentable.

She had to pick out the right combination of shirt and pants, shoes that matched, etc., etc., etc. He agonized daily over his sock drawer, unable to decide on color or style. It was driving her crazy.

His name was Irving Gavelman, and he was even worse at breakfast. He couldn't decide on eggs or toast, pancakes or waffles.

"Should I carry my umbrella today or not?" he wondered out loud one morning, as he changed his socks for the third time. "Should I call Mother tonight or tomorrow night? Maybe I'll take the bus to work today after all. Or should I take the car?"

Eileen pushed him out the door and collapsed in a sigh.

How could such a spineless, unassured mouse make demanding, life-and-death decisions day in, day out, as a judge in criminal court? It was beyond her.

Their relationship had always been a thorn in her side. She recalled with derision their early days as newlyweds.

Over breakfast they'd decide to go out for dinner later in the evening. All day Eileen had to sit on pins and needles, waiting to see if her lawyer hubby would come home from his cases victorious.

If so, they'd go out. If not, she would be subjected to his ranting and raving as he'd emotionally argue against the dinner idea. He'd storm back and forth, jabbing his finger at her and pleading his case. The only way to appease him was to give in and stay home and eat leftovers.

She'd had it. That night when he came home and asked her what show they should watch on television, she spilled her guts. She told him she was tired of him, that she didn't want to make his decisions for him any longer.

She forced him to sit down and go over the books to determine how much money they had in their accounts. He nervously scratched out the figures and pushed the paper toward her. She eyed the numbers like a madwoman before making a pronouncement.

"Irving, starting tomorrow, I'm quitting my job and becoming an alcoholic," she said firmly. "We can afford it, and it's what I've been wanting to do for some time."

"But, Eileen," he appealed. "You don't even like to drink."

"I'll learn to like it," she said. "We can live on your income, and we'll sock away some money each week in case I fall down a flight of stairs or something. If we plan ahead everything should be all right." She grinned at her flabbergasted husband.

"Don't I have a say in this decision?" he asked.

"Fuck you, Irving," she said.

A Dogcatcher's Tale

Umberto Switney couldn't keep a job because he performed his tasks too well. As dogcatcher for the community of Grievous Junction, West Virginia, he was fired on his first day on the job when he returned to headquarters seven times with his truck loaded with runaway mutts.

"What the hell are we supposed to do with all these damn dogs?" railed his boss, Yubetcher Drizzledorfer, allergic to fleas to begin with.

Umberto drifted on to Grant's Rectum, Virginia, where he was appointed to the double post of highway commissioner and city clerk. His first act as highway commissioner was to order his workers to reconstruct the bump on Highway J that had been worn smooth by the traffic.

"We can't just remove the "BUMP" sign and store it in the city garage," he told his employees. "What a waste of the taxpayers' money that would be."

But if his underlings didn't care for his ways, they didn't have long to wait before he once again made his own bed and fell out of it. He proposed to change the name of Grant's Rectum to "Construction Ahead."

"We'd get double the use out of the signs that line our streets," he explained. "Save a lot of tax money." They ran him out of town on a rail.

"Nobody's going to change the name of this town," said Alfred Jenkins, 83. "I've lived here all my life. I'll be damned if I'm going to die in some strange place I've never even heard of before."

The Fifth or Sixth Beatle

Merv Whittington was a sluggard and everybody knew it. After dropping out of high school in 1960, he bounced from one low-paying job to another, trying to find excitement, or at least fulfillment.

He landed in London, England, in 1963, and promptly found employment as an errand boy and part-time reporter for the news tabloid *The London Rag*. Using cutthroat tactics, he worked his way to the top and turned the paper into a shameless sleeze publication almost overnight.

Compelling headlines were the order of the day, every day. "To hell with the stories themselves," Merv always said. "It's the headlines that sell papers."

"Aged Adolf Hitler Discovered Teaching Kindergarten in Ipswich," "Queen Elizabeth Thinks She's Winston Churchill," "Prince Charles Switched at Birth, Is Really Snot-Nosed Orphan." Truly, to *The London Rag*, nothing was unbelievable.

Trouble hit one day, however, when Merv went too far with one Brian Epstein, manager of the up and coming rock band, The Beatles.

The headline read, "Beatles' Manager a Woman in Drag—Is Subject of Band's Songs." The *Rag* reported that Brian Epstein's real name was Sally Baconrind and that the band's version of "Long Tall Sally" was a tribute to him/her.

Songs like "She's a Woman," "I Wanna Be Your Man," and "Do You Want To Know a Secret?" suddenly became more intriguing. The *Rag* said "I Saw Her Standing There" drew its inspiration from the time Brian forgot to lock the door of the shower at their hotel in Hamburg. And the excrement really flew with the report that "I Want To Hold Your Hand" was in reference to Brian/Sally's prosthesis, which nobody knew about either.

Enraged, Epstein vowed to settle the score, but before he could, Merv Whittington found religion.

He fell hook, line and sinker for a traveling holy man making the rounds. The Maharishi Ooshi preached love and forgiveness, gentleness and joy. His real name was Al Donnigan and his roots were similar to Merv's. Hailing from

Moose Jaw, Saskatchewan, Al was a high school dropout looking for an easy road.

He instructed Merv to make amends to those he'd offended and lead a life of peace. Merv folded the *Rag* and walked directly to Brian Epstein's office to see what he could do to garner his forgiveness.

Brian was no fool. Seeing an opportunity, he told Merv he'd forget all slights and slanders if he'd agree to perform a rather enviable duty.

The Beatles were to leave soon on a tour of the States. Brian wanted Merv to be the Beatles' stand-in. With his thinning hair and bulb-like proboscis, Merv looked a little like Ringo with the mange and would have to be fitted with a Beatle wig. "We'll glue it on with plastic cement and if you slouch a bit, from a distance you'll pass for any of them," Epstein assured him.

Seeing this as an easy way to put himself in the Maharishi's good graces, Merv jumped at the chance. Only later did he realize the realities of the job.

He was brought along to act as a decoy. Shoved to the floor of the Beatles' limo, when the hoards of screaming teenage girls got to be too much, he was tossed out the door. By the time the girls realized he wasn't a bonafide Beatle, the real Fab Four were out of sight.

Each time it was the same. Initially pawed, kissed, caressed, and fondled, to his horror he wound up beaten, kicked, spit at, and lambasted.

He persisted at it only because he'd met a girl named Connie who was head-over-heels in love with the Beatles, and he thought he could win her over if he could only convince her that he was their friend and confidante.

He gave up on her finally. "Forget it, Connie," he fumed. "There are other fish in the sea, you know." And he was right, there were.

But all of them were in love with the Beatles, and none would believe that their fab heroes would have anything to do with such a sluggard of a schmuck as Merv Whittington.

Crooked Hero Worship

It was no secret that Vernel Schmigg, third grade teacher at Lincoln Elementary School in Muskegon, Michigan, loved and worshipped ex-president Richard Nixon. Indeed, one of his first items of business upon gaining employment at the school was to replace the classroom portrait of George Washington with one of Nixon that he'd purchased some years earlier.

No one seemed to mind. His co-workers thought it odd that a seemingly intelligent man would do such a thing, seeing that it was now 1993 and Nixon was little more than a relic of history, but it didn't really matter to them.

The few parents who visited were either mildly pleased or couldn't have cared less. The principal, Clendon Dulpepper, was too busy putting out the small brush fires that kept cropping up all over the place to even notice.

But over the years strange reports circulated. Was Vernel Schmigg indoctrinating the children with the ideologies of Richard Nixon and the old Republican guard?

Vernel had become a Young Republican in 1968 only because he had nothing better to do and thought he'd meet good-looking women. By 1973, his fascination with the president had become hero worship.

It enraged him to see his beloved president embroiled in an embarrassing scandal. Watergate and Nixon's eventual fall haunted Vernel Schmigg through the years and into 1993.

If the Lipschitzes hadn't moved to Muskegon when they did, things might have continued on into oblivion. Jerry and Connie Lipschitz were hippie holdovers from the sixties. Their only child was unfortunately placed in Vernel Schmigg's classroom at mid-semester.

Sunbeam Snorkel Lipschitz (Connie had given him his first name, and Jerry, who was into snorkeling for a while, provided the middle) was a harmless lad, rather precocious, but not obnoxious about it. He wasn't the problem. His parents were.

When they showed up for a parent-teacher conference and spied the grim countenance of Richard Nixon looking down on them, they screamed bloody murder. They raised a stink that wafted all the way to the administration building, where the school board sat in session.

An investigation followed, but despite rumor and speculation, nothing solid could be pinned on Vernel Schmigg. There was no proof of anything shady going on. As Nixon had been president, his portrait on a school room wall could not in itself be construed as scandalous.

Forever after, however, Principal Clendon Dulpepper was on the lookout. One false move would be enough for him to immediately oust Vernel Schmigg. "I can't afford any bad publicity at this point," Dulpepper rationalized over dinner with his wife, Dooley.

Then the dark day arrived. Sunbeam Snorkel Lipschitz ran home with the news that Mr. Schmigg had hissed during a boring social studies lesson, as if unable to contain it any longer, "Our country needs Richard Nixon again!"

The Lipschitzes were there in a second, threatening sit-ins and spewing 60's vernacular. Clendon Dulpepper, sweating bullets, promised prompt disciplinary action.

But on questioning Vernel Schmigg, he realized again that he had nothing on him. It was the kid's word against his. The principal needed conclusive evidence.

The next day before school, Principal Dulpepper crawled into a cabinet at the back of the classroom and waited. When Mr. Schmigg and his students filed in, Dulpepper listened with his ear pressed to the cabinet door, his pocket tape recorder whirring away.

It was a waste. When Vernel Schmigg finally turned out

the lights and went home at four-thirty, Clendon Dulpepper rolled himself out of the cabinet and uncurled himself stiffly.

Determined, he tried again the next day. And the next. Finally, the following Monday he hit paydirt.

Shortly before three, Mr. Schmigg told the kids to put their math books away. He shuffled to the door and locked it. He lowered the window shades.

He stood in the front of the room and in a low voice told the kids, "Someday the history books will be rewritten and Richard Nixon will take his rightful place as The Father of Our Country!" A distinct thumping emanated from the back cabinet as the dismissal bell rang. The kids filed out.

"Mr. Dulpepper?" asked Vernel Schmigg with a smugness you could cut with a dull butter knife.

"Let me out of here!" came the muffled reply.

"I'll have you out in a minute," Vernel Schmigg said calmly, knowing the jig was up. Clendon Dulpepper struggled angrily with the stuck latch. All he could think of was the look on the face of the PTA president were she to come in on a remote chance and see him like this.

Vernel Schmigg jimmied open the door and, having the principal scrunched vulnerably inside the wooden cubicle, promptly reached in and strangled him.

"There was nothing else I could do," he rationalized as he lugged him to the incinerator in the boiler room. "He would have turned me in, sure as shit."

Back in the classroom, Vernel Schmigg found Mr. Dulpepper's tape recorder on the floor by the cabinet. That evening at home he played back the tape.

Hearing himself spout on about Nixon being "The Father of Our Country" made him grin with pride. The ensuing thumping, struggling, and heavy breathing of Clendon Dulpepper brought a shiver to the spine of Vernel Schmigg.

He listened with a cool detachment to the verbal exchange between himself and the helpless man in the cabinet, then gritted his teeth as he listened to the coughs and sputters of the dying man.

Vernel Schmigg considered erasing the tape to wipe out any evidence that might be used against him. But he reconsidered, tossing the tape into a dresser drawer before falling off to sleep.

Hildegard the Temptress

Gooder N. Thow, self-taught philosopher and part-time religious zealot, hot on the motivational-speaking circuit, lounged in his room at the Sugary Suites Hotel in downtown Shreveport one hot August night. He was to speak at nine the following morning in a conference room somewhere in the bowels of the building, and now he was thinking.

"What new statistics can I add to my spiel for tomorrow?" he wondered. He'd been running the same facts and figures, catch-phrases and jingles, percentages and statistics, past his audiences for weeks now. It was time for some fresh data.

"Hmmm...Let's see. Upon looking into the mirror, eighty-nine per cent of the general public thinks at least one negative thought. 'I'm ugly.' 'My eyes are too close together.' 'I'm getting old and gray and wrinkled and disgusting.' 'My jowls need tightening.' 'I'd be beautiful if I'd just get that new permanent I saw in *Facade* magazine.'

"Interestingly, if allowed to stare for five seconds, the number climbs to 93%. If given 20 seconds, they think of something to hate about themselves, and the number jumps to 96%.

"That leaves two per cent who are incurable narcissists, one per cent who are mentally slack, and a half per cent who are too sleepy or drunk to care. The half per cent remaining is made up of people with optimistically healthy outlooks on life, but don't stand there too long, even you!"

He scribbled all this on a note card, utterly disgusted with his sloppy handwriting. He looked out at the city lights and mentally scraped the bottom of an empty barrel for new insights. Then inspiration hit him like a brick in the center of the forehead.

"Rise to any challenge," he said with a headache coming on. "Don't back down from a challenge...Hmmm." He knew he was onto something special, close to formulating a new slogan for his next tour.

"Don't back down because you can't go down back."

That was it. He could see himself exhorting the huddled throngs to take on life's challenges, look them in the eye, back them into a corner, and beat them into submission, if not utter oblivion.

"Once you've come to the end of the road, you can't go down back," he said, smiling. He liked the sound of it. He jotted it down and headed for the hotel pool to take a midnight swim.

He had the whole pool to himself except for a fat, uneducated woman lolling about at the far end. Intent on ignoring her, he dove in and backstroked a frothy path down the center of the pool. As he passed the woman standing in waist-deep water, he heard her garble something, and he reluctantly stopped.

"What did you say?" he asked.

"Would you teach me how to do that?" she said unpleasantly.

"Well," he said, clearly hesitating.

"I've always wanted to do that," she complained. "I could never get my arms and legs to jibe at the same time."

Groaning within, Gooder N. Thow glanced at the clock.

"Don't they close the pool soon?" he asked.

"It's open 'til one A.M.," she frowned.

"Well, I'd really like to help you but I've got an early morning ahead of me and—"

"You shouldn't turn down an opportunity to help another

human being," she scolded and his own words rang in his ears. *Rise to any challenge*, he thought with dread. *Don't back down, you can't go down back.*

"All right," he said. "Let's start by having you hold onto the side of the wall here and kick your legs in the water." The woman, who went by the name of Hildegard Sloane, gleefully kicked and splashed, doing it all wrong but making up for it in enthusiasm.

"If someone had taught me this at an early age I wouldn't have gotten so goddamned fat!" she giggled.

"Weight loss is all in the attitude," Gooder intoned. "Sixty-five per cent of all people who purchase diet books don't need to lose weight," he said, making up statistics as he went along. "Ninety-seven per cent of all people who lose at least ten pounds on a diet, gain it back within a year. If they'd use the power of the mind, they'd—"

"Bullshit, it's all in the metabolism," Hildegard Sloane panted, still kicking up a splash at the side of the pool. She might as well have bitten off his tongue. He said no more for the rest of their time together, choosing instead to listen to her fascinating ideas on mental and physical health and fitness.

When the custodian kicked them out at one, Hildegard was no closer to being able to backstroke than when she'd started. But Gooder was enraptured by her raw humanness. They shared a pizza in his room and later, after he cancelled all current bookings, fled to Mexico to be wed.

They spent their days eating greasy hamburgers and chocolate eclairs, getting fat, and enjoying every minute to the fullest.

For Lydia, Wherever the Hell She Is

They all remembered Son of Sam, the New York City madman who sent notes to the police after his gruesome murders of young women and their male escorts. Now, years later, with that killer safely locked away, similar homicides were being chalked up by the N.Y.P.D. And there didn't seem to be any rhyme or reason to them.

*Merlin Shwinby, 45, unmarried shoe salesman, found shot in an alley two blocks from his home in Brooklyn. The murderer wasn't interested in his wallet or the two hundred dollars folded neatly within.

*Norm Tremayne, 66, retired house painter, found shot in his car in an underground parking structure in Manhattan, murdered in broad daylight.

*Leslie Trindl, 43, insurance processor and property appraiser, strangled with an extension cord in the basement of his home in Great Neck.

*Wally Huberton, 51, real estate hack, clobbered with a board too many times to mention, in his garage in Brooklyn.

*Benson Greeg, 56, custodian at P.S. 155, shot in the chest in the front hall of his home in the Bronx. His wife Hazel found him there upon her return from a visit to the dentist.

*Calvin Eubanks, 60, wealthy investor, stabbed repeatedly with an ice pick in the parking lot of a fashionable night spot in the Wall Street section of Manhattan.

"There are no clues," lamented Inspector Claude Nein. "There don't seem to be any connections at all. We could just sweep them into the unsolved wastebasket if it weren't for the fact that at each murder scene we've found the same message scrawled on a 3 by 5 card: 'I Love You, Lydia!'"

"WHO'S LYDIA?" the headlines read. No one seemed to know.

It took a rookie cop, Kiley von Schwiebel, to crack the case. He was the one who noticed that all the victims were either bald or had an ever-widening bald spot.

They recruited Sgt. Wilbur Dreck, bald deskman from the eighth precinct, to act as decoy for an ambush. Half the force pounced on Eric Queeley in Central Park when he moved to knife Sgt. Dreck, squealing pitifully, "Lydia! Lydia!"

They had their man and Kiley von Schwiebel got a hero's welcome wherever he went, whether he was coming or going or not.

Eric Queeley had been unhappy in love, spurned disgracefully by Lydia Buttgrind because he wasn't bald. Hopelessly infatuated by men with shining baldspots, Lydia couldn't stand the sight of Eric and his thick, shaggy mane and she told him so.

Looking Down on Darling Murgatroyd

Carl Dongreco-Bobbalonia groaned getting out of bed, calling on every ounce of will power he could muster. It was 3:20 in the A.M. and, as usual, he had to take a leak.

Like never before, he was sorely tempted to just piss in bed and clean it up in the morning, so tired was he. "But," he reasoned, mumbling in his thoughts, "I've got a headache anyway. I might as well get up and take an aspirin now to save time in the morning."

He crossed the hall to check on the baby first. Little Murgatroyd breathed softly, like a baby angel sleeping on a cloud. Carl sighed lovingly and tucked him in around the edges.

He trudged down to the bathroom, puzzled to see the light on within. He pushed open the door only to find a large, grim-faced man sitting on the toilet with his pants down around his ankles, doing what one does when one is in such a position.

Startled beyond all composure, Carl turned to leave, then realized this was no public restroom where he'd accidentally imposed upon some stranger. This was his own house in the middle of the night.

"What are you doing here?" he gabbled.

"I wandered in and had to take a crap," the stranger said, staring evenly at the man in the flannel pajamas.

"The doors are locked."

"A window was open," the stranger said.

"But how can you do such a thing?" Carl asked in disbelief.

"I don't have any problem with it," the stranger said calmly.

"Without an invitation?" demanded Carl, his shell softening with each calm response from the stranger. "What if the house had been a mess?"

"It looks fine to me," the man said.

Carl scanned the floor and the bathroom sink. He had to agree the place was rather tidy for once.

"Well, thank you," said Carl, so starved for compliments he'd take them from anybody, anywhere.

"It's cold in here though," the stranger complained with a mild shiver.

"Should I turn up the heat?" Carl asked. He was beginning to like the visitor and was grateful for the company (his wife hadn't talked to him since their spat over who got to eat the last slice of the meatloaf).

"No, don't bother," the man said. "I won't be long."

"Would you like something to eat? Or drink?" Carl gave the stranger a hopeful look.

"No," he said. "No, thanks."

"So where are you from?" asked Carl as he pulled up the clothes hamper and sat down. "I haven't seen you before. Are you from the area?"

"What's with the nosy questions all of a sudden?" the stranger responded testily. "Leave me alone."

Crestfallen, Carl got up and plodded back to bed, his bladder about to burst. He drew the blankets over himself, then angrily threw them back off and made his way back to the bathroom to insist that the stranger at least have the decency to answer his questions while using the facilities in his own humble abode. But when he got there the man was gone.

With a tremendous feeling of sadness, Carl Dongreco-Bobbalonia shuffled back to the baby's room and looked down on darling Murgatroyd.

"Hurry up and learn to talk," he pleaded tearily. "Someone around here needs you." The baby stirred with dreams of annoyance, awakening in the morning immersed in a cranky mood.

Carl's wife, Matilda, was even worse when she found the mud on the bathroom floor. Carl listened to her wailing and screeching as he sat eating a breakfast of grief, his feet freezing on the cold kitchen floor.

Knuckles, Nails, and Fingers

Knuckles, Nails, and Fingers were hit men employed by the Vito Grandiosity Family, New York, New York, U.S.A.

Knuckles (real name: Angelo Largento) came across as a quiet, unflappable sort, but beneath the surface lay a powder keg with a short fuse. He followed directions implicitly, making him Vito Grandiosity's favorite employee. He preferred the use of his bare hands over any firearm or incendiary device, hence the nickname.

Nails (real name: Tony Olivecasserole) was a thug, no more, no less. His most distinguishing feature was his broken nose, bent like the broken legs of his victims (fractured kneecaps were his trademark). He was tough, tough as nails.

Fingers (real name: Luther Coswell) was unlikable. Even Vito Grandiosity himself got the creeps being around him. He had long fingers and played the piano in his spare time.

As per Vito's orders, the three lived together, taking turns on most of their assignments, although collaborations were sometimes necessary. Brawls and slugfests were common occurrences among them, much to Vito's annoyance. They simply couldn't stand each other.

Indeed, they had just two things in common. First, they shared a blind devotion to Vito Grandiosity. And second, they liked to watch old reruns of *The Donna Reed Show* at two o'clock on weekday afternoons. That's where the trouble started and that's where our story really begins.

When Boyd Derlock, station manager at WZYX-TV, made the decision to revamp afternoon programming, he had no idea what turmoil he was about to bring upon himself.

A meek, balding man in his mid-30s who weighed 155 pounds holding a ten pound weight in each hand, Boyd thought he'd been around the block where rerun-programming was concerned. After all, wasn't it he who axed *McHale's Navy* last year in favor of *The Phil Silvers Show,* bringing on a storm of furious fan letters?

When Knuckles, Nails, and Fingers came pounding on his door, Boyd Derlock assumed it was his secretary with his morning doughnut and coffee. He'd been trying every angle to get her to go out with him. This morning he wore only the skimpiest in male swimwear, hoping to entice her with his trim but lumpy muscles.

"Come in, Miss Slathgart," he called, pirouetting in front of his desk, giggling with glee. His mood changed when the three gorillas tramped in, sneering at his get-up.

"Uh," Boyd stammered. "Wh-What can I do for you…uh…gentlemen?" He ducked behind his desk and pulled out a shirt from the top drawer, covering himself as the three crowded around him.

"We wanna know whatcha got against Donna Reed," snarled Fingers.

"Yeah, we don't like *Let's Make a Deal,*" hissed Nails.

Knuckles grabbed Boyd Derlock by the collar. He pulled him clear out of his chair, belched into his face, and said, with a tooth missing, "You get Donna Reed back on the TV by tomorrow or you'll never walk again."

"And that's if you're lucky," added Nails. Without another word, they dropped Boyd into a heap on the floor and departed.

The next day *The Donna Reed Show* was back on the airwaves and Vito Grandiosity was furious.

"Where'd you fellas go yesterday morning?" he asked, his blood boiling within.

"We took care of Big Willy O'Malley the way you told us to, boss," said Knuckles.

"What else did you do?" the kingpin barked.

The three roughnecks looked at one another nervously. Vito didn't need any further information. He whipped out a machine gun and sprayed them full of lead.

"I happen to like *Let's Make a Deal*," he said with a sneer as he stepped around the bodies, tiptoeing over the rivulets of blood spreading across the floor.

An Author's Self-Appraisal

As usual, morning came too early for Smyrl Crogan, but he got up anyway. And, as usual, he found himself sitting at dawn in the wreckage of the night.

He was an erstwhile famous writer, but of late his books had been creating logjams at the book stores. No one bought them anymore.

His last work, *The Juice is Always Oranger on the Other Side of the Lunch Counter*, sold a sluggish thousand copies or two and now collected dust on the racks of bargain book shelves and resale shops.

If only he could recapture the uninhibited spirit of his blockbuster bestseller, *My Life Inside a Bucket*, in which he described his experiences living with his head inside a plastic bucket for more than a year (it opened with the line that stirred a generation: "It was yellow.").

"But I'm a good relative," he said to himself as he washed

his feet in an aluminum pan on the back porch. He sneered at a singing bird. "They can't take that away from me, for Christ's sake.

"I visit them when they're in the hospital or something… What more do they want from me anyway, goddammit?"

The Man from Nantucket

There once was a man from Nantucket who worked for the Prince o' Peace Holy Card and Bible Company, Inc. He went by the name of Julius Q. Fishtitz, and day in and day out he tramped his way back and forth on the assembly line, checking to see if the staples were in straight or if anything looked to be out of order.

It was the ultimate in drudgery, which was what initially attracted him to the job, but it had now become tiresome. He tried to jazz up the place by scrawling dirty limericks on the men's room wall but after being reprimanded by his superiors, Monsignors Francis Godom and Ronald Somorrah, he decided to refrain, at least until the job situation in Nantucket brightened somewhat.

His resolve, however, lasted only a week or so. Monsignor Somorrah hit the roof when, taking a leak, he discovered another piece of Julius's doggerel.

"I just can't stop," the exasperated man intoned upon being grilled by the management in a small dingy office. "I honestly had no intention of doing it, but something comes over me when I'm in there. It's the humidity. Or the scent of the soap powder…I don't know. I need help…"

But the monsignors were neither compassionate nor patient. They fired him without another word of warning.

Julius Q. Fishtitz landed right side up though, gaining employment with a rival card company that recognized his special insights and rhyming ability. They provided him with a private toilet stall and a painter who whitewashed the walls each night after quitting time.

Having a clean slate on which to scribble each day, Julius's creative genius flowed uninhibitedly. The holy card verses he wrote reflected his newfound tranquility and wisdom.

His cards inspired young and old, rich and poor, and, long after the Monsignors Godom and Somorrah had passed away and gone to hell, Julius Q. Fishtitz still turned them out, day after day after day.

Personality Profile of Rimpole Blang

Rimpole Blang took the corner on two wheels, the tires of his tomato-red Mercedes screeching in agony. He slowed the vehicle, revving the engine, as he approached a dainty young woman striding purposefully down the avenue.

"Pretty snazzy, eh, Toots?" he said with a wicked leer.

"I beg your pardon," said the prudish miss.

"Come off it, sister," Rimpole snarled. "Play your cards right and I'll take you for a little spin. What say?"

"No thanks," she said, stalking off in a huff.

"Your loss!" he crowed nastily, roaring off, blazing spark plugs and all.

He reached into the bag on the seat next to him and shoved an entire hamburger into his mouth, just to indulge the urge. He gulped it down and tore into another, tossing the wrapper out the window as if it didn't matter.

"Hey, you assholes!" he hollered to a small crowd of teenagers standing on the corner. "If you're trying to keep that slab of sidewalk from floating away, let me tell you something! It's cemented to the ground!" He gunned the engine and, leaving a cloud of exhaust and a patch of rubber, was gone.

It was Rimpole Blang's lunch hour and he was spending it the way he always did, kicking up his heels and blowing off steam. He cranked the stereo to maximum volume and sped up the street. Spying a fragile old woman struggling with packages at the crosswalk, Rimpole revved the car into high gear.

He rocketed toward the helpless woman and hit the puddle at 50 mph, dousing her but good. He laughed snidely and his eyes twinkled as he checked her out in the rearview mirror.

Glancing at his watch, he was sorry to see that his lunch break was nearing its end. He zoomed up the street, over the bridge, and into a different neighborhood, where he slowed down to a respectable speed and combed his hair into place.

He pulled his car into the parking lot and walked to the clean white building where he worked. He passed a few colleagues and nodded soberly as he made his way down the hall to a comfortable room with bland paintings on the walls.

Checking his notes, he rose to greet his first client of the afternoon. He ushered the woman in and, after they both were settled, began the questioning.

"Tell me, Mrs. Rosewell. When did you first find yourself engaging in the self-destructive behaviors you described to me last week? And were you able to follow my advice and conduct yourself in a manner consistent with your status as a high society doctor's wife and mother of three, or did you give in to your impulses and follow through with your plan to sexually take on the entire motorcycle gang you've been chumming around with?"

Nun of the Above

I
The Bishop's Decree

Back in elementary school, we had a nun of the above. God loved her and the feeling was mutual.

She questioned us about our after-school activities but we didn't mind. We openly told her the truth except for an occasional pack of lies.

She was as nutty as a squirrel, as she herself knew as well as anyone. Everybody laughed at her behind her back, then cowered in fear of reprisal.

She had a damned dog named Ezekial who shat on the convent carpeting, leaving stains where no one wanted to see them. The other nuns complained.

The bishop heard of the nonsense and turned a square shoulder to it, at first. But they pestered him and he gave way, forcing our nun to rid the convent of the unholy beast.

II
Not as Much Fun and Twice the Bother

The dog wandered, grew frustrated, and bit a man on the leg. Years earlier, the man had met the father of the nun of the above in an old diner, though neither remembered.

Back at the convent, the nun of the above was like Jell-O in turmoil. She missed her dog and began to fidget and almost frolic.

The other nuns felt bad for her but, didn't openly show their feelings. Still, they worried about our nun. She was different now—not as much fun and twice the bother.

Growing increasingly testy, our nun finally left the convent, walking out to the byway to hitch a ride to nowhere in particular. Her dog happened to be wandering in the opposite direction but she didn't know or else she would have turned around and walked the other way.

Our nun, who was called from above at the age of six, repeated herself as she tramped on the shoulder of the byway, no one offering her a ride. "Damn," she said.

III
Both Had Hidden Pasts

Our nun of the above met Henry eventually. They settled in a small town far from home. Together they began a new life, for both had hidden pasts.

Henry was older than our nun and thereby had advantages and disadvantages to take into account. He'd been a school janitor, fired and wandering like our nun because he'd let white walls turn gray and lunchroom floors get sticky. He was perturbed with nuns because one had fired him but after meeting our nun, things were never the same.

They were deeply in love and thoroughly enjoying it. The two of them went everywhere together. They slept at night in the same large bed and even used the same identical toothbrush in the morn.

IV
The Dog's Nazi

Ezekial wandered aimlessly until he was captured by a man named Gosnold, who thought he was Adolf Hitler. They became great friends, especially after the dog convinced Gosnold that he wouldn't bite him.

Gosnold took the dog to Nazi meetings and German memorabilia gatherings. The dog loved the meetings, especially when all the Nazis gave him pats on the back.

The man and the dog went on trips and travels of all varieties, including one to Hollywood, where Gosnold won thousands of dollars on a TV quiz show. They lived high on the proverbial hog between then and the time all the money was gone, which was four weeks later. Gosnold gave most of his prize earnings to the Nazis, foolishly.

The dog could no longer conceal his disgust and bit Gosnold in the leg. Then he continued wandering.

V
Mending Their Ways

Henry had been treating our nun well until he accidentally slapped her in the face while trying to slap himself in a fit of chronic self-hate. She ordered him off the premises, to which he refused. A horrendous fight ensued.

Finally, a minister convinced the two to remember their wedding vows and what the priest had said: "I now pronounce you man and wife in jolly matrimony." Our nun and Henry reconsidered their plight and shook hands as friends.

"Thank goodness we were reminded of those wedding vows," our nun said and Henry agreed all over himself, although there had been no such vows—Henry and our nun had never been married.

"Let's mend our ways hereafter," said Henry who, although on a diet, continued getting fatter.

VI
A Ghost of a Tramp

Our nun's dog found himself in a damp cave inside a mountain, whimpering for his estranged Nazi friend. By some odd quirk of chance, however, an old convent hymn recycled itself inside his head, providing him with the spiritual strength to venture forward into nothingness.

Soon he found himself hustling through an old forgotten railroad tunnel that led to the other side of the mountain where the weeds and grasses grew into his eyes, obstructing his vision.

As the dog continued scampering forward blindly, he heard a sound that enticed and intrigued. Up ahead, on the side of the abandoned railroad track, sat the ghost of a tramp playing a lively dulcimer, waiting forever for a train to take him back to his old stomping grounds in the city trash yard.

Our dog had found a new friend and wagged his tail appropriately. The two became intimate chums immediately. The bum told the dog tales in the dark, spicing up the stories with dramatic twists on the dulcimer. The dog loved the music and howled to the moon.

They curled up at each other's feet and slept the night away. The bum awoke bright and late, next to the snoozing dog. When the dog awoke his friend was gone.

VII
Vehemence and Violence

Our nun of the above and her lover Henry lived together without incident for awhile. They respected each other a lot, though grudgingly.

The nun only made matters worse by matter-of-factly stating that Henry did not have talent enough to get on television someday. As this was his lifelong dream, the news was devastating, causing him to experience stomach cramps, for which he sought relief through swallowing Citrate of Magnesia.

"My sponsor someday!" he yelled to the nun between moans and complaints, holding the bottle high for all to see.

She helped him into bed, soothed him, and wiped his saliva. She mistakenly assumed that this was an opportune time to tell Henry that she was pregnant with a baby on the way. Since she was only kidding, it didn't really matter that he reacted with vehemence and violence.

In the middle of Henry's tirade, the doorbell rang. A woman was in need of help with car repair.

She used their telephone but dialed the wrong number, so her husband drove off and helped someone else with trouble of equal magnitude. The lady expressed her eternal gratitude anyway before leaving.

VIII
Zigzagging to Oblivion

The dog narrowly escaped the clutches of a dogcatcher but was oblivious to the fact, so it's just as well. He zigzagged across the wild and woolly terrain of South Dakota, in search of a scent of some kind that would give him at least a minimal clue as to what he should be doing at any given moment.

IX
Rest and Relaxation (but No Eggs)

Our nun's Henry tried for a career in writing but it didn't work out. His prose was overladen with cliches and his poetry was littered with couplets that had "puddle" rhyming with "what'll" and other such abominations.

In contemplating chucking his dreams for drudge work after all, he considered momentarily what Spiro Agnew might advise in a situation like this. Then he remembered it was 1990, not 1970, and Spiro Agnew wasn't even in the news anymore so it probably didn't matter what he thought anyway.

Our nun wanted to force Henry to go on a small vacation to sort out his cluttered mind. He said he'd go if they could stay in a hotel and not in the tent she'd pilfered from the basement of the convent the night she left.

"I'm not sleeping in some creepy old nuns' tent," he declared.

"Then maybe we'll just stay home," she said. "You know I don't trust hotels. At least at home you know how clean the beds are. Not very."

Henry won her over in the end, and they enjoyed their stay at the Hairy Arms Hotel, at least until breakfast the next morning when Henry discovered the hotel had bacon but no eggs.

"You gotta have one with the other," he whined. "If God had wanted bacon and eggs to be separated, He'd have made them that way."

X
The Crossing of the Paths

Our nun and Ezekial, destined to wander the continental terrain like two roving comets in infinite space, crossed paths without knowing it on August 18, 1990, outside the Hairy Arms Hotel.

The dog sniffed at the bases of the signposts on the front sidewalk until he was chased away by the attendant whose job it was to sweep the area at nightfall. Down a back alley Ezekial roamed, into the night.

Henry strode out of the revolving door, loaded down with ready-to-burst suitcases filled with what-not and what-have-you. Our nun trailed behind, lugging a crate that had arrived in the morning mail.

"We'll take it home and then open it," Henry declared. "It will give us something to look forward to." Our nun could have agreed more but didn't.

Henry helped her load the crate into the taxi's trunk. She turned to get into the back seat of the car but didn't make it without incident.

When no one had been watching, Ezekial had left a pile

in the gutter and our nun's purposeful stride landed her squarely into the midst of it. She angrily scraped the substance onto the adjoining curbstone, much to the dissatisfaction of the sidewalk attendant, who rarely had to watch for such deposits from the likes of civilized human beings.

Of Reptilian Descent

Bernard Bebendiquinn Reptile slithered as he crept from his office in downtown Squatts Flats late in the month of May.

"It's too damn hot," he grumbled, and he meant it. He was as dry as a saltlick in a drought.

"I must get to water," panted Bernard, trudging down the streets of Squatts Flats toward his home in the flophouse apartments above the laundromat.

Bernard keyed the door and burst in, panting and wheezing. He found relief in his bathtub, the water cold, filling his gasping pores.

Bernard Bebendiquinn Reptile had been living in Squatts Flats for thirteen years without anyone finding out the disgraceful truth: Although he was an amalgam of flavors both ethnic and national, being partially English, French, German, Swiss, Swedish, and what-not, he was, to his great shame, of reptilian descent as well.

Somewhere on a distant branch of his family tree there'd been some cross-breeding done by a lonely ancestor who worked the railroads out west. The result for all offspring ever after was the curse of a horrible affliction of dry scaly skin, relieved only by total immersion in water.

And, since his brother Langley had been found dried up and dead on a subway in New York (another of the countless awful deaths diligently recorded in the family yearbooks), Bernard was the only one left.

"Gads," mumbled the unhappy chap, sitting at the kitchen

table with a wet towel around his shoulders, green around the gills and gray on the underbelly. He leaned to the right and snagged the remainder of this morning's muffin off the cupboard with his lightning tongue.

"Ah, shit," he said, fighting off another craving for dragonflies.

They Died with Their Clothes On

Shortly before they were married, Carla and Vernon Honeywinkle agreed they would never argue. If they ever did find it necessary to interact in a quarrelsome way, said the dreamy-eyed lovebirds, they'd do it in the nude.

Needless to say, occasions of arguing arose once their pleasure boat of marital bliss hit the rocky whitewater of real life. At the first hint of displeasure from either party, both would immediately disrobe and the argument would officially begin. Early on, when their bodies were young and supple, these nude altercations consistently led to quick reconciliations, capped by lively romps in the honeymoon suite.

As they grew older and more tired of each other, however, they learned to make up quickly, simply because the resulting romps were becoming time-consuming and bothersome.

"Okay, you're right," Vern would spit as Carla angrily pulled off her blouse. "Damn it!"

Obviously, they had to be careful with their marital discord while in public but you can't foresee everything, and one day they couldn't help themselves, being absolutely fit to be tied with each other in a department store in downtown Tollgate, Oregon, when they hit a snag while shopping for a new television set. Vern wanted the model with remote control, Carla was dead set against it.

"For God's sake, Vern," she hissed, much to the embarrassment of the store clerk, who was incredibly hen-pecked himself. "The only exercise you get is getting up to change the channels!"

They dragged each other to the restroom area, where they found the men's room empty. They locked themselves inside the farthest stall, seething with anger as caustic as acid.

Vern hoisted Carla up on the seat so her feet wouldn't be visible, and Vern kept his socks and shoes on and let his pants fall around his feet so everything would seem normal in case an intruder stumbled in. So as not to attract undue attention by arguing even in hushed tones, they dashed angry messages to each other on a scratch pad Carla kept in her purse for just such emergencies.

They ended up compromising, filled with great disgust for each other. Vern got to have his remote control but he had to agree not to use it on Sundays, Tuesdays, and Thursdays, so he'd get at least *some* exercise.

Eventually they spent their days just sitting there, saying nothing out of fear of starting something, trying to avoid arguments at all costs. If, heaven forbid, tempers did flare and Vern's suspenders came flying off in a hot fit of rage or Carla unzipped her frock with the frenzy of a rabid animal, one or the other would come to their senses and admit they were wrong.

Their contempt for each other increased at the same pace as their revulsion for the sight of their sagging bodies, bodies that had hair growing out in places neither of them knew existed back when they were younger.

This mutual indignation and utter loathing for each other kept their love alive and vibrant, and their relationship on the cutting edge of passionate longing, far beyond the normal span for a typical husband and wife.

The Chronicle's Chronicle

James Jacob "News" Prynt had had a nose for news all his life, hence the nickname given by classmates on the school yearbook staff. He nosed about in newsrooms in between semesters at journalism school and eventually found steady work at an unsteady daily, *The Chronicle*.

It was only a matter of time before "News" Prynt wormed his way into managerial positions, then onto the editorial board. And when Snufflepuss Pendingdon Adams, age-old senior editor, sickened and died like a pickle in a barrel, "News" Prynt was chosen to succeed him.

All went well for several years, until "News" Prynt was overtaken by what many called crazy ideas.

"It's the same news every day," he bellowed to his staff at their weekly meeting. "I'm sick of it and I bet our readers are, too."

Some months before, "News" Prynt had stopped reading the news altogether, so sick of it was he. The sports and business pages were okay, and the gossip columns, horoscopes, and comics he read with abandon as always.

But a fondness for the interesting fillers appearing at the ends of columns buried in the inner pages of the paper took hold of him and, seeing the potential for a revolution in news coverage, "News" Prynt ordered a flip-flop in the space given to news coverage.

The blaring headline the next day was, "85% of the World's Peanuts are Grown in Africa and Asia." Buried at the end of the Community Calendar on page 8 was a filler: "Congress Overrides Veto of Tax-Cut." "That says it all anyway," "News" Prynt contended with a wave of the hand and a satisfied smile.

What used to be fillers became special features. "No President Was Ever Born on the Third of the Month." "Halley's Comet, Last Seen in 1985-86, Will Return in 2061-62." "In Some Places, Yak Dung is Used as Fuel For Fires." "A

Musical Instrument Called the Didgeridoo Has Been Played by Australian Aborigines For Thousands of Years."

And tucked within were the fillers: "Earthquake Rocks Venezuela—600 Dead." "Gas Station Attendant Found Murdered—Suspect in Custody." "Secretary of State Resigns in Shame." "Governor Embroiled in Messy Affair With Wife's Hairdresser's Sister."

Sales boomed, the stock soared, and "News" Prynt was named Man of the Year in the year-end issue of *The Chronicle*.

A Man Ahead of His Time

Lawrence von Schmiddler walked the streets of Bonn one cold bright morning in winter. His self-confidence was written all over his long, loping strides, his morning porridge strewn all over the front of his shirt, unbeknownst to him, of all people.

He loped on through the doors of an old storefront on the west side square. The sign read "Schulzbocker and Sons, Publishers."

"Good day, sir," Herr Schulzbocker cried from behind a cluttered desk. "What can I do for you?"

"I have something here," Lawrence said, unwrapping a bundle of bent and wrinkled papers. "It's a TV script."

"A TV script?" the old man said, peering with a frown at the mass of wadded paper on the counter.

"Yes," von Schmiddler said with pride. "I am hoping you can find a buyer."

"TV?" asked the puzzled Schulzbocker.

"You know," said Lawrence. "Television."

"It hasn't been invented yet," Schulzbocker said.

Lawrence von Schmiddler crinkled his brow sadly and departed. His discouragement got the best of him and he bought six eggs from a wandering peddler. He stalked to a house two streets away and pelted it, leaving six gooey splotches of yellow on the wall facing the street.

Whenever he felt low, throwing eggs at this house was good therapy. It belonged to Lawrence von Schmittler, who created great havoc in Lawrence von Schmiddler's life due to the similarity of their names.

Von Schmiddler bristled with extreme resentment when strangers about the city of Bonn mistook him for von Schmittler, who was nothing but a lowly street sweeper.

Lawrence's TV script sat on the shelf for a week before he walked the three blocks to Schulzbocker and Sons to try again. Being turned away was disheartening, but he would not be defeated.

He tried every week for more than two months, hoping they could connect him to someone, somewhere, who might want a TV script. By now Lawrence von Schmittler was understandably annoyed by the weekly egg splotches on his wall.

Finally, Schulzbocker had had enough. When the little bell tinkled above the door one morning, and Lawrence stood standing there again with his stupid smile and baggy cheeks, the book publisher let him know, in no uncertain terms, just how he felt.

"Listen here, you," Schulzbocker started. "For God's sake, it's only 1848. No one's even close to inventing the TV yet. You're wasting my time. Now get the hell out of here! And don't come back!"

Lawrence hung his head and trudged back home. He tore up the script and threw it in the fire.

He decided to take his writing talent and go into the more conventional career of novel writing. He was doomed, however, due to the lagging book sales that greeted his first published work, *The Losers Are Winning*, an epic description of the rise and flounder of 18th century Austria.

"Why would I want to read a book written by a street sweeper?" the customers said. It wasn't long before the shopkeepers removed the book from the shelves.

Eventually, Lawrence von Schmiddler lay dying, still believing that TV script-writing was his forte.

"It's a shame no one helped me out by inventing it in my lifetime," he thought as life drained out of him like piss from a leaky toilet.

Temporarily Quiet on the Internal Front

Lloyd Quagmeyer lay in bed on a peaceful Friday night, glad to be finished with work for the week and glad to be alive. Feeling like a wrung-out wet rag, he closed his eyes and listened as his wife, Whutta, greased her face with cold cream at the bedside vanity.

The Quagmeyers had recently moved to Stumprot, Michigan, from Chicago, Illinois, mainly to get away from the noise of the big city.

"Aaaah," sighed Lloyd, pulling the covers up to his chin. "Ain't it nice?"

"Sure is peaceful, ain't it, Lloyd?"

"It sure is," the man said, a smile twisting his tired face.

"Remember the noise of the city?" asked Whutta, daubing her eyebrows with some kind of white paint that was to help in preventing them from turning gray or falling out.

"Oh, God," groaned Lloyd. "The traffic, the buses, the el!"

"The yelling, the music, the sirens."

"That god-awful factory, pounding away at our sensibilities every second of every day."

"This was the best thing for us," said Whutta, tweezing out a stubborn hair on the flap of her second chin.

"Listen," said Lloyd wistfully. "You can hear the tolling of a church bell."

"Ain't that nice?" said Whutta absently.

"And far away I hear the lonely sound of a train in the night. Who knows where it's been or where it's going next?"

"Hm-mm."

"And it must have gotten foggy since five o'clock. You can hear the distant, steady drone of the fog horn from down on the docks."

"Ain't that nice?"

Minutes later, Whutta, having smeared her face thoroughly with black goop, reached over and switched off the light. She pulled a clear plastic bag over her head so as not to stain the pillow cases and, after situating her nostrils over the breathing holes, crawled into bed next to her hubby.

She listened as the fog horn kept up its muffled, distant chant. She heard the heavy iron church bell peal away melodically. Melting into a dream, another train called from the still of the night.

Whutta Quagmeyer was suddenly jolted from her slumber by Lloyd tossing his sheets one way and rolling the other, then turning and elbowing her solidly in the ribs.

"Lloyd, what's the matter?" she cried with alarm.

"Well, how can a person sleep with all this fucking noise!" he yelled, his teeth clenched like steel traps, his blood pressure at the bursting point.

It doesn't pay to run when you just can't hide.

My Darling Little Brother in an Ankle-Length Dress

When Alice Hornswaggle found herself widowed at the age of 38 with seven boys to raise, the last thing she expected was to meet someone who would tickle her fancy at the funeral.

"Oh, why didn't Maurice trim his beard periodically like

other bearded men?" she sobbed into her sister Gladys's shoulder. "Why did it have to get caught in the machinery at the factory? Why didn't one of his co-workers carry a scissors?" These and other questions ran through her mind relentlessly.

As she shivered and wailed on her way out, she spied Verhag Bavier standing on the periphery, his eyes downcast but nevertheless gleaming. He had come from Colorado to visit his sister Gwegan and her family, and to stay for a week or two.

When he arrived on the afternoon bus, Verhag was quick to sense the tension sizzling on the surface. The joyous reception he'd expected wasn't to be; instead, icy hugs were given all around.

"Ralph's pissed," Gwegan explained as she buttoned up the kids' sweaters. "A guy he works with got killed and not only does he have to work overtime tomorrow night and miss the hockey game on TV, he has to go to the frickin' funeral tonight." Not knowing what else to do, Verhag decided to tag along to the funeral, just to be with everyone else.

It was love at first sight. Verhag saw in Alice someone who could possibly handle his omnipersistent sexual needs. She saw in him someone who might be able to whip her seven sons into shape.

It wasn't long before she was "in the family way" once more, this time hoping desperately for a girl. Verhag didn't help matters by falling to his death from a rope bridge in northern Ontario while camping with friends.

Now more than ever, Alice longed for the days when life was much simpler, when you didn't have to lock your door at night, when neighbors helped one another, when she wasn't a single mother trying to raise seven kids with another on the way.

She found herself getting lost in old reruns of *The Andy Griffith Show* on a daily basis, shushing the kids and neglecting her housework. She especially enjoyed episodes that featured Aunt Bee, played by seasoned actress Frances Bavier. Alice often wondered if her late husband might have been a distant relative of the actress.

As time went by and her pregnancy continued, Alice's desire for a girl grew more tenacious, and she set her decision to name the baby "Frances."

Imagine her horror when it turned out to be a boy after all. Sick with despair, she named the ugly little brute Francis with an "i," and let it go at that. Or so she thought.

She couldn't shake her dream of having a girl. She was tired of black leather and motorcycle parts, beer cans and cigarettes, baseballs, basketballs, and *Playboy* magazines. She didn't want another truck driver, army man, auto mechanic, or iron worker in the family. She wanted frills and ribbons, laces and bows.

When Francis turned four, Alice threw away all his jeans and flannel shirts and bought him his first dress. The older boys balked but Alice snarled at them like a mother bear protecting her cub, and they backed away with furrowed brows.

Little by little, Alice groomed Francis into the ways of Aunt Bee. He learned how to cook, how to dust and mop, how to tie his hair into a bun.

When oldest brother Arnold scraped his chair back from the dinner table one evening and made movements toward the door, little Francis piped up with a cheerful, "And where do you think you're going, young man?"

"I'm goin' to work," he answered dourly.

"Not until you've finished your beans," said the little tyke with a shake of the head. "Mom and I didn't slave over a hot stove to have food wasted. And you'll finish them with a smile," he chided, pouring more milk for brother Claude.

"Ma!" Arnold appealed, his hands spread wide in supplication.

"Ma!" Claude begged, his voice lined with contempt.

"Ma!" all the other brothers pleaded.

Ma looked away with a satisfied smile, giving little Francis the tacit approval he'd come to expect.

"Tut, tut," he said, pointing to Arnold's empty chair, fixing him with a gaze that made his flesh crawl. Arnold slinked back to the chair and forked down the rest of the beans before fleeing out the door, down to the iron docks.

For a while, the boys sat glumly on the porch when they weren't at work or playing sports with their rough and tumble friends. They couldn't bring anyone home anymore, lest they get a scolding from Little Brother for leaving a banana peel on the kitchen table or not wiping their feet on the front hall rug.

But they adjusted. What else could they do? They sat and watched *The Andy Griffith Show* together, took to calling Francis "Aunt Bee," and mended their messy, macho ways, much to Alice's eternal delight.

Dinner or Death

There he sat in his La-Z-Boy recliner, waiting for dinner or death, whichever would come first. Custer Darvillion, old and spent, hoped his wife, Darlene, would hurry with the dead bird she'd popped in the oven so long ago.

Custer and Darlene had lived long and fruitful lives, raising four run-of-the-mill children, toiling away at the Jameson Textile Plant until their hands were permanently dyed an off-magenta, and taking their rightful turns as chairmen of various committees for the Jaycees of Floral Print, South Carolina, their beloved hometown. Now it was time for their just desserts, but the rest of society wasn't cooperating.

"The president called today, threatening to gouge our Social Security checks again," Darlene announced as she flopped on the couch. "Dinner will be ready in a minute."

"You know, we made a big mistake letting Junior get

married," Custer wheezed.

"I know," his wife agreed. "Now he spends all his time with his wife and kids."

"Doesn't even seem to think about us anymore," the old man said.

"Well, we've got to make do with what we've got," said the ever-optimistic Darlene. "You know what my daddy used to say: Today is the first day of the rest of the week."

"Yeah, yeah, I remember," Custer said with annoyance. He'd heard it all before. In fact, the two of them had had this exact conversation just yesterday, twice. "When will dinner be ready?"

"Momentarily," Darlene replied, "if not sooner. You just relax and stare at the walls. I'd better hurry. I've yet to write that birthday card to my ex-husband's dead wife's mother. Maybe I can fit that in before the chicken is done."

"What time is it?" asked Custer, his voice laced with irritability. "I can't decide if I'm tired or not."

"It's a little after seven, but don't drift off. Dinner'll be ready before you know it."

Later he sat, still waiting. "I wonder what my ancient ancestors were like?" he said to himself. "Probably a bunch of assholes."

On and on he waited. He wished now that he'd gone to the $150-a-plate fundraising dinner for world hunger down at the school gymnasium.

Waiting for a dead chicken made him feel even more insignificant than he already was. No one was waiting for *him*.

He was less important than a bird that had been murdered, beheaded, defeathered, gutted, frozen, thawed, coated with flour and spices, and placed belly up in a hot, steamy oven, surrounded by shriveling root vegetables.

Dinner or death, which would it be?

"For Christ's sake," Custer said with a quizzical brow. "Aren't there any other alternatives?"

Wasting Away Again

Matilda Hornsby was in trouble again. This time she was arrested for improper disposal of a nontoxic waste, a misdemeanor so rarely enforced that Sergeant Bulge of the Crooked Foot (Iowa) Police Force had to hunt the back pages of the manual to get a handle on what to do.

The water company complained to the police that it was finding blobs of mucous-like slush in their intake valves. "Someone is responsible for this," said head water man, Lucius Leekenspray, with an astuteness not often found in such a place as Crooked Foot. They traced the problem to a west side neighborhood, where the police began inquiring door to door.

Matilda Hornsby had been in trouble with the police before. She'd misunderstood the concept of parking tickets when she first began to drive, thinking the tickets she found on her windshield entitled her to free parking privileges in the downtown area. Only after she compiled over $600 in fines and was tossed into jail did she learn the bitter truth.

Years later, at the height of the baseball card-collecting craze, she was arrested trying to pass herself off as Rogers Hornsby's granddaughter at a collectors' show, charging twenty dollars per autograph.

She was tripped up by a twelve-year-old boy who noticed she was signing, "Matilda Hornsby, descendant of Roger Hornsby."

"Whoever heard of someone naming their kid *Rogers*?" she yelled as they dragged her from the bench to her new home in the county facility.

But that was years ago.

Now, when the police knocked at her door to ask questions, she was in the middle of repapering her bathroom. Several probing questions led to the ultimate truth: Matilda Hornsby found it easier to flush the old wallpaper wads down the toilet than to lug it to the trash out back.

"Ma'am, the water company has complained," the cops said. "You'll have to come with us."

"Am I being arrested?"

"Yes, ma'am. You'll be spending the night in the slammer."

"I don't blame them for complaining," she admitted on the way. "I knew it was hideous wallpaper. That's why I was taking it down."

Death and Taxes

Ima and Arnold Dufus sat down to do their taxes on a cold Saturday night in February. Neither had ever had the pleasure of tackling the job before.

In years previous, Ima always left the task to her domineering husband Carl, who had passed away unregrettably, shortly after the last tax collection.

Similarly, Arnold left the tax-paying duties to his wife, Polonese, who always had a way with numbers. She died the previous May when her brain unexpectedly hemorrhaged while working on some particularly difficult math problems with her teenage grandson, Buzz.

Ima and Arnold were married in August and now were stuck with each other at tax time. Ima did most of the work due to Arnold's chronic daydreaming, but she didn't seem to mind.

"Is it customary to tip the IRS?" asked the old woman, her pen ready to ink in the amount owed.

"I don't know," Arnold said, his forehead crinkled with uncertainty. "I guess maybe it is."

"Fifteen per cent?" she wondered.

"That'd be safe," Arnold said with a reassuring nod.

When the payment arrived with the note explaining the 15% tip, the IRS men were in nothing short of a dither. The president himself was summoned to present, in person, a notice that the Dufuses were to be admitted to the Taxpayers Hall of Fame, a little-known establishment just up the street from the Smithsonian in Washington.

There were so few inductees the entire business was housed in a room the size of an overgrown broom closet. Most of the registrants' identities were kept secret, being people who were never told they'd accidentally overpaid on their taxes. Their names were kept on microfiche in a large black box labeled "Donations of the Unknown Taxpayer," hidden in a vault under the floorboards.

Alas, when the president arrived to make his presentation, the Dufus home was in flames, the two cringing in a corner somewhere, inhaling deadly fumes. The Secret Service insisted on what it calls 'presidential right-of-way,' so the firetrucks had to stand aside and wait.

When word got out that it was the president's limo causing the traffic snarl, Harlington Tydippin Knotts, an ordinary joe who happened to be walking by at the time, summed up everyone's feelings when he drawled, "The president's a nice guy, really. If he just weren't such an asshole all the time."

The Rumor Mill

At long last, Elwood V. Pumpanickel had scraped together enough money to act upon the idea that had come to him in a hazy dream one vicious, restless night so long, long ago. He proudly gazed up at the blinking neon sign that hung over the bustling sidewalk in downtown Salem, Oregon.

"The Rumor Mill," it read, and Elwood was open for business.

His first customer was an elderly man who wanted to know if it was true that Lawrence Welk had died and, if so, was his death in fact attributable to an overdose of illicit drugs?

"My estimate is that I will find the information to confirm or debunk your rumor within twenty-four hours, with minimal expenses incurred," droned Elwood, trying to make the recitation sound routine. "Therefore, I set the price at fifty dollars, of which a deposit of half must be made at this time."

"Here's my twenty-five dollars," said the man, whose name coincidentally happened to be Pierpont Welk, although he wasn't related to the famous bandleader. "I'll be back tomorrow at this time for my answer."

"Your deposit will be cheerfully refunded if I am unable to provide you with the data."

The next day Mr. Welk breezed into The Rumor Mill on pins and needles. Elwood V. Pumpanickel gave him a smile and a hearty handclasp.

"Did you find anything out?" asked Pierpont Welk with bated breath.

"Yes, I think you'll be quite pleased," said Elwood. "First, the bad news is that the reports of Lawrence Welk's death are in dispute. Ever since this Elvis thing, my job has been awfully difficult. There's an unrelenting rumor coming out of North Dakota that says Lawrence is still alive and playing a conga drum in a rhumba band in Colombia.

"Other alleged witnesses claim to have seen him at Kentucky Fried Chicken establishments in various cities around the country, and there's one annoying rumor, persisting for quite some time, that he's been seen buying Geritol at a Walgreen's in Kalamazoo.

"Unfortunately, I cannot dispute these claims with absolute certainty, as that would be virtually impossible. And since there is always a chance that these wackos are right, I need to preface my statements with a warning to that effect.

"However, you may rest assured that a large body of evidence shows that Lawrence Welk died at his home in May of 1992. There is no evidence that he ever used illegal drugs."

"Thank God for that," sighed Pierpont.

"Yes," Elwood agreed. "Causing unexpected trouble in my investigation, however, was an interesting phenomenon I call 'predestined anachronistic expiration.' It occurs when someone gets so old that most people assume they're dead when in reality they're still alive and kicking. This occurred in the life of Lawrence Welk at least twice, documented.

"The first was a small smattering of rumors arising in southern California around 1975 that had Lawrence dying of natural causes at the age of 72.

"The second was a widespread belief brought to light in 1983 that he'd passed on some years before. A poll taken at the time showed that, nationwide, 84% of those interviewed thought he was no longer with us. This confusion in the minds of so many made it doubly difficult to reach a definitive answer for you, but there'll be no extra charge.

"I did uncover another rumor in the process of my investigation that proved to be quite interesting. Apparently, back in the late sixties, Lawrence Welk and Jane Fonda carried on a steamy, behind-the-scenes love affair.

"The initial weekend trysts on the beaches of South Pacific islands gave way to furious arguments about U.S. foreign policy, which brought the blossoming relationship to a grinding halt before it could develop into anything serious.

"Once again, it didn't take much to prove that these stories were complete fabrications, but I thought I'd throw them in as a show of my thanks for coming to The Rumor Mill."

"Thank you, ever so much," Pierpont Welk said with a grin, and he paid his fee in full, walking out into the afternoon drizzle breathing easier and feeling like a million bucks.

Later that same day, a frumpy middle-aged woman named Doris Ajarr entered with a question that had been burning within since she'd heard it at the hairdresser's last Tuesday.

"Is Ann Landers really just a made-up person who fronts for a board of old men who like to dole out advice to the confused? Could it really be true, as one woman claimed, that

Ann Landers is really Ernest Borgnine and that, in between movies and other engagements, he writes the column because it gives him further creative release?"

"Hmmm," Elwood said, wheels turning. "I estimate it will take three to four hours of phone calling and digging through the archives to arrive at your answers. My fee will be thirty-five dollars plus long distance calling charges."

"Fair enough," Doris said with a relieved smile. She dropped a twenty on the counter and promised to return the following afternoon. When she arrived at the appointed time, Elwood was up to his ears in paperwork, busy as hell, but he had Mrs. Ajarr's information.

"If you worked in this field as long as I have, you'd know that rumors are like meat. You can grind it up and make it into something different, like steaks into ground chuck, but in the end, it's still just meat.

"Rumors don't usually materialize from nothing. They might get a little chewed up in the process, sometimes to a point where they're no longer recognizable, but there's usually a basis of fact.

"Your rumor about Ann Landers is a good example of this. I don't know where the story about Ernest Borgnine came from. As far as I can ascertain, Ernest Borgnine is Ernest Borgnine, no more, no less.

"Evidently, someone got mixed up between Borgnine and Bob Keeshan, the man who played Clarabelle the Clown on the old *Howdy-Doody Show* and later the character of Captain Kangaroo on children's TV.

"Of course, a woman named Eppie Lederer is the front for Keeshan, but he's the mastermind behind Ann Landers. He was quoted through one of my sources as saying that the two personae, Ann Landers and Captain Kangaroo, complement each other perfectly. 'Doing one without the other would have driven me crazy long ago,' was what he said.

"Interestingly, Ann's counterpart, Dear Abby, uses a similar approach. Clearly, writing an advice column takes a toll on a person's psyche, and emotional releases are imperative. Dear Abby blows off steam by doubling as—now you might not believe this but I have evidence—Minnie Pearl."

"Thank you very much," Doris Ajarr said with a delighted laugh as she clunked her checkbook down on the counter. "I can't wait to tell the girls."

Elwood V. Pumpanickel ran a brisk business verifying and discrediting rumors concerning everything from all-night drug-induced pillow fights among Hollywood's elite to NASA's discovery of JFK's brain tissue in a jar on the surface of Venus.

But he hit the big paydirt only when he began contributing items to the supermarket tabloids. Through his customers he had an endless source of preposterous stories, so, unlike the other tabloid headline writers, he didn't have to burn himself out with hallucinogenic drugs to get his ideas.

Hilgarth Iksnubble, Are You an Asshole?

Wally Rimjob, thirty-seven years old and aging steadily onward, tucked the paper bag under his arm and walked briskly to his car. He'd just purchased more tropical fish and wanted to get them home before they died, as was their wont whenever he bought them.

As he approached his car parked at the end of the block, a screeching squeal of tires jolted him from his thoughts. He turned in time to see the collision of a snazzy yellow Corvette and an old, overused Chevrolet. He winced at the explosion of metal and glass and hurried to offer assistance to any who might need it.

A young man with permed hair and sun glasses leapt from the Corvette and ran circles around the car, frantically inspecting the damage.

"Oh, damn!" he cried. "Look at my car!" *Hmmm... Which of us is he addressing?* Wally wondered as he moved to the other car to see if the passengers were all right.

Inside the old Chevy were a young mother and her two children, ages one and three. They were shaken but not hurt. The mother held the little ones, who wailed in fear and shock.

The police were on the scene in a minute, asking nosy questions and scribbling incessantly into official notebooks. The man answered all questions tersely, eyeing his wreck with great sadness. Not once did he offer a word of any kind to the family in the other car.

Wally stayed on the scene, forgetting about the delicate lives in the bag he was holding. He watched with interest as the Corvette driver was given citations for speeding and reckless driving.

Wally sneered at the man when he remarked to anyone who would listen, "Now my insurance will go up again." And he observed with keen interest the clerk who had sold him the fish just minutes before, rushing from the store crying, "Boss, what happened?"

Later that night as Wally sat and watched his sick-looking fish swim around the tank, he took stock of his feelings.

"I'll never buy fish from Noah's Tropical Emporium again," he said with determination. "It's a lucky thing I witnessed that accident today. Now I know what kind of a jerk owns the place."

But in bed that night a thought nagged at him like a rusty nail in his shoe. What about some of his other favorite stores? Did he know any of the owners? They might be even worse than the jerk in the Corvette. He'd have to do some research.

In the morning, Wally flipped through the Yellow Pages, intent on finding out about these mysterious people behind the scenes.

"Daddy, the fish are all floating at the top of the tank," his little daughter Hortilda informed him.

"Not now, honey," he said with distraction as his fingers

punched in a number on the telephone.

"Hello," said the usual nasal voice on the other end. "Butler's Boots, Belts, and Other Belongings. Can I help you?"

"I'd like to speak to the owner, please."

"Mr. Butler? I'll see if he's in yet." After a moment's pause, a deep, gentle voice spoke into the phone.

"This is Robert Butler."

"Mr. Butler, this is Wally Rimjob. You don't know me but I've been a customer of yours for at least twelve years. I just want to know, what kind of a guy are you?"

"Well, I think I'm a nice guy," he said without hesitation. "My wife and kids would probably back that up. I've got a lot of money but I try not to be obnoxious about it. I give some to my church and I buy cookies from the Girl Scouts every year. Stuff like that. I try not to get on people's nerves, and if I use the last of the toilet paper, I try to remember to replace it for the next person."

"Fair enough," Wally said. "Sounds good."

The next call was placed to the owner of the Wild Flower Country Club, where Wally golfed during the milder seasons of the year.

"Could I speak to the owner of the club, please?"

"I can put you through to his office in the back," drawled a woman who sounded like she'd put morphine in her coffee at breakfast. "Hang on."

"Hallo," growled the voice of Hilgarth Iksnubble.

"Hello, my name is Wally Rimjob. I golf at your club ten or twelve times a month and I guess I just want to know what kind of a guy you are."

"Well," Hilgarth said with a touch of annoyance, "I ain't too many people's favorite person. I don't pay my help much, and I got a short fuse with them most of the time. My wife left me long ago and took my home, my best car, and the kids. I tried to dodge my child support payments but she put the sheriff on my tail.

"I don't know. A long time ago I told myself, stop being

such an asshole, but it's easier said than done.

"At least my brother Hathbart drinks like a fish and has an excuse for people hating him. I don't drink. What people get is pure, unadulterated me. I guess you'd have to label me a first class asshole if there ever was one, when it comes right down to it."

"Well, thanks for the information," said Wally Rimjob cheerfully as he scribbled sown the data.

By the end of the day he had a complete list of establishments he could feel free to patronize, as well as one of places to avoid.

Washed up on the Beach

George Willikers sat old and lonely on a bench near the beach, watching the kids run amok. Goldarn Gnitt approached, wobbly cane and all.

"Nice day," Mr. Gnitt said with a smile.

"Not bad," George responded. "But with southwesterly winds and a dew point of 80, I wouldn't be too sure."

"Yes, there are some ominous cirrocumulus clouds that have been building since mid-morning in the east."

"They may be inconsequential," said George with a wave of the hand. "More important is the fact that the barometer has fallen steadily since midnight. There is a warm front blowing in from Iowa, though."

"I heard there's a high pressure system holding over northern Indiana," Goldarn pointed out.

"Is that right? This morning's weather report predicted highs in the seventies but I'll have to see that to believe it..."

Four hours later

"Yep, those clouds have moved out for good," Mr. Gnitt said with a smile, leaning back on the bench and putting his feet up on the retaining wall.

"I knew they would," said Mr. Willikers. "We've had less than three inches total precipitation all spring."

"What did you think of last Thursday's humidity levels?"

"Oh, it looked like we were in for some uncomfortable weather but it only lasted, what?"

"About 36 hours."

"Yeah, and if you live in this part of the country you've got to expect a day like that once in awhile."

"That's a fact. The sky sure is getting gray to the south..."

Two hours later

"The winds off the lake are making the air temperature lower than in the inland areas," George said, his voice growing slightly hoarse.

"That's true," said Goldarn. "According to my trusty pocket thermometer, today's temp peaked at 67 between 2:30 and 2:45."

"Is that so? I remember a time, was it in '46 or '47? The temperature was 82 and within an hour it fell to 38. Such are the changing weather patterns of south-central Wisconsin."

"I wonder what's causing this gradual darkening of the skies we're experiencing at the moment?"

"Hmmm. I hadn't noticed. Perhaps a storm system is moving in from Illinois."

"More likely it's unstable cloud cover caused by falling barometric pressure."

"Would you two shut up and go home?" said Mark Honck, muscular lifeguard and aspiring lounge singer. "It's eight o'clock, it's getting dark, and the beach is now officially closed."

Father and Son

There was no sense in continuing the discussion.

Bondurant Gleeg paced the floor furiously, kicking at imaginary objects as if they were there.

Everything had been said. There was nothing left with which to feed the flames. He wasn't getting anywhere. It was obviously a total waste of valuable time.

But he carried on anyway.

"Son, you've got to reconsider," the red-faced man wheezed. "Why can't you listen to reason? I've been around the block a few more times than you. This just ain't right."

"Dad," said Lynn "Gweeny" Gleeg, "I only know what my heart tells me. And I know with Lula it's the same. We're going through with this."

"But, son, you're breaking your mother's heart. Don't that mean nothing?"

"I feel for Mom, but my confidence in this whole affair wins out. Someday—I just know it—Mom will feel different. So will you."

"But, Lynn," railed the old man. "Don't you realize what this means? Your life will be turned upside down."

"I'm looking forward to it, with or without your blessing."

"But, son," cried Bondurant, tears welling up in his bloodshot eyes. "You're nineteen and she's eighty-seven!" He tried to say it with a disdain that could not be ignored.

"We will be happy together," Lynn insisted.

Bondurant gazed at the floor, his nerves crawling. "I don't think your mother will be able to take it, if you want my frank opinion," Bondurant continued. "She's always wanted grandchildren, you know." The young man said nothing.

The two sat enveloped in stillness, like a couple of weary soldiers in the wreckage of battle. Bondurant ran his fingers through his graying hair, then rubbed his forehead to ease the tension there.

"Ah, son," he said with a sigh. "You just don't know. At your age, it doesn't matter what your old parents are feeling.

"The people at my office are starting to talk. They clam

up when I walk in but I know they're talking about you and this scandalous situation."

Lynn stared at his father with a horrified glaze in his eyes. His mouth was suddenly dry, too dry to produce the words that had jumped to his lips. He swallowed hard.

"Dad," he said. "The people at the office, are they really, you know, talking about Lula and me?"

"Yeah, son, they've been whispering about it behind my back for some time now."

"Oh, my God," groaned the horrified young man, shaking his head and staring into space.

The whole thing was called off. Bondurant Gleeg went back to holding his head high at the office. Lynn buckled down and lived the rest of his life on the straight and narrow.

Lula found someone else.

Little Babies Playing a Boys' Game

It was a beautiful day for a ball game, the Angels were on the field, and the visiting Red Sox were being introduced via the stadium loudspeakers. The crowd was in a tizzy not just because of pennant fever (it was, after all, only May 29), but because of the fact that Jerome "Swats" McDonald, record-breaking centerfielder for the home team, was selling popcorn in the stands as per the directions of the team's owner.

"He can't play again this year because of that toe injury," the old man said with a repulsive cough. "I'm paying him six million a year on a guaranteed contract. We've got to get *something* out of him."

"His agent says he'll file suit if we force him to sell anything heavier than hot dogs," said the young flunky. "They're afraid he'll aggravate the injury."

So he was selling popcorn and the crowd hoped for a glimpse of their hero.

The game dragged on, zero to zero, into the sixth inning. Angels' pitcher Sneaky Fingers threw three straight balls to the Red Sox's weakest hitter, Slub Pockmark. Catcher Vance Rollaway jogged out to the mound for a conference.

"Sneaks, you want to go out for a cold one after the game?" the burly young catcher growled.

"Sure thing," Sneaky replied.

"Maybe we can call our wives and have them meet us at The Stadium Grill for dinner."

"Sounds good to me."

The crowd tittered nervously as Sneaky Fingers fired the next pitch. The ball was hit to left field for an easy out. Two batters later the count ran to two and two. Again Vance Rollaway called time-out and trotted to the mound.

"Do they have a special tonight at The Grill?" he asked.

"I don't think so," Sneaks said. "Not on Saturdays."

"I thought they had some kind of a deal with all-you-can-eat."

"They've got a chicken plate, four pieces for $6.95. It's all you can eat, unless you pay another $6.95 for another four pieces."

"You're probably right," the catcher said with a nod.

The game resumed. The Angels scored six runs in the bottom of the eighth to give them a seven run lead going into the ninth. With that kind of a lead, all were surprised when again Vance Rollaway trudged out to speak with his pitcher. The count on Craig Knox was one ball, no strikes, with two out.

"Sneaks, I forgot my wife is visiting her sister today in Long Beach. Maybe we could make a night of it ourselves. Ask a few of the guys if they want to come along…"

The fans started to boo the delay.

"Hmm, let me think about it," the lanky pitcher said thoughtfully. "I guess it doesn't matter to me."

"Well, it don't matter to me either. You decide."

"Play ball!" bellowed the umpire like someone with a nasty toothache.

"Listen," said the catcher. "When I get back into position, I'll hold down one finger. That means you want to call your wife. Just nod if that's what you want. Otherwise shake me off. If you do, I'll give you two fingers. That means you want to ask some of the guys and make a night of it. All right?"

Sneaky nodded, but confusion set in before the catcher got back to the plate. Did he say one meant he'd ask his wife? Or was that two?

When Vance Rollaway put down one finger, the pitcher nodded without knowing exactly what he was nodding for. When he pitched the ball, he was still in a state of confusion.

The pitch had nothing on it, a floater that loomed over the plate as big as a beach ball.

Unfortunately for Craig Knox, it was late in the game and as usual he had the cocaine jitters something fierce. He swung at the ball with a round-house swing, missed by a mile, and swung at it again. Out.

After the game, the sportswriters clambered all over Sneaky Fingers and Vance Rollaway, asking questions and needling them with their astute observations.

In the paper the next day the two were praised for being "driven by competition," "skillfully honed to perfection at their craft by a single-mindedness of purpose," and "gifted with a burning desire to outperform all, against all odds."

Indeed, they persevered through difficult times behind in the count, amid rambunctious, sometimes-abusive fans, with temperamental coaches, managers, and owners breathing down their necks. Like Spartan warriors, they battled to the end.

All for a lousy paycheck.

Hard Times with His Daughter's Father

Melrose P. Diddywiddy awoke one summer morning

with a hard fact chasing him into the caverns of his mind. He pulled the covers over his head but there it was, probing and pricking at his consciousness, like a needle at an overinflated balloon.

He tried to hide in the closet but it followed him, taunting and teasing, until he almost burst with frustration and pain. He ran through the living room, hollering at the top of his lungs in an attempt to drive it out.

It was no use. He gave up and, while sitting piteously in a crumpled heap on the cold kitchen floor, faced the truth by saying aloud, though no one was there, "I am deathly afraid of my neighbor's judgment."

To drive the point home to any disbelieving subpersonalities lurking within, Melrose walked to the front window and gazed out with reddened, tearful eyes.

Across the way, his neighbor, Clark Goodman, tall and handsome, strong and straight, happily busied himself with raking and pruning, typical pastimes for a summer morning.

With a shudder, Melrose watched as Clark Goodman swept a pile of clipped branches into a wheelbarrow and prepared to dispose of them properly.

"My grass has needed cutting for days," Melrose said with shame. "I don't even own a weed-eater. I don't fly a flag on holidays or put up Christmas ornaments in December. I don't go to church. My books are always overdue at the library. My life's a mess."

Melrose P. Diddywiddy hung his head and cried, his tears falling to the soiled carpet.

"What must my neighbors think?" he moaned. "I can't show my face. What if one of them made a derogatory remark?"

At least his daughter, Rosewater, gave him pride, he mused with a thin, uncertain smile. He had momentarily forgotten, however, that she'd run off with that steel guitar player, Anthony Grinnderswitch, and was now making the rounds of the TV talk and gossip shows under the name of

Rosewater Diddywiddy-Grinnderswitch, promoting her bestseller, *When the Shit Rises and You're There, You Know You're in the Toilet*, about her crummy upbringing and how she overcame it.

Melrose was furious with her now but he missed her nonetheless, so he turned on *The Drew Jeers Show*, listening as Rosewater described a childhood filled with persecution, deprivation, and guilt. As any father would be, Melrose was immensely proud of his daughter for having the spunk to get on national TV and speak with such poise.

He cursed Clark Goodman, whose roaring lawn mower drowned out her last sentence before the commercial, causing Melrose to have to reach for the remote, resulting in a crick in the back that lasted for three weeks and counting.

A Day in the Night

Ed Barnsnubble, stomach oozing over the waistband of his checked boxer shorts, plodded to the bathroom in the darkness of three o'clock in the morning. Much to his surprise and relative delight, he didn't trip or step on any clutter on the floor in the hall.

Half asleep, he pushed open the door and stepped inside, only to find himself hurtling into an abyss, dark, dank, and seemingly bottomless. Someone had removed the bathroom floor and all that was under it.

"Aaaaaaaah!" he screamed, his voice trailing off like a train whistle in the night. Then all was silent.

"Ed?" called Merva from the warmth of their bed. "Ed?" There was no answer. "Oh, for Christ sakes," she complained as she whipped on her robe. "What the hell happened to him now?"

Merva stormed down the hall, her bristly legs flexing with anger, her face pinched with disgust. She stormed into the bathroom and, reaching for the light switch, sputtered, "Ed, what the—Aaaaaaah!" She too plummeted into the darkness.

Ed, Jr., barely conscious, reluctantly roused himself from a dream about the new neighbor lady and groped for his bedroom door.

"Ma?" he called. "That you?" There was no answer, other than his sister Clarice asking sleepily from her room down the hall, "Eddie, what's going on?"

"I don't know," the rugged young teen replied. "I thought I heard Ma. Down by the bathroom." He tramped his way down the hall, cursing mildly upon tripping on the vacuum cleaner hose.

"Ma? Dad?" The bathroom door was open and all was dark within. Puzzled, Ed, Jr. stumbled in.

"Aaaaaaah!"

Clarice, age twelve, stood at the door of her room, listening to the stillness of the big, drafty house. "Eddie? Mama? Daddy?"

Gingerly stepping around the strewn junk she'd grown accustomed to, Clarice made her way to the bathroom. "Eddie?" she called quietly, as if not to puncture the silence. She stepped inside.

"Aaaaaah!" she screamed, falling through the air like a rag doll in the wind.

The Barnsnubbles lived the rest of their days in the Home For Waylaid Families, eating nothing but gruel day in, day out, except for porridge on holidays.

Model Citizens Come in All Shapes and Sizes

In 1883, the city fathers of Cambridge, Rhode Island, named the newly donated tract of land "Judacus Pernelli Smith Park" after a future war hero, leaving money in an account for a statue when such a person was deemed fit to be honored.

Many families with last name Smith tried to fulfill the wishes of the old council, naming their sons Judacus Pernelli, but none rose to fame as foot soldiers or medics, let alone generals or joint chiefs.

Finally, in 1972, Russell Calliope Biederbaum, mayor of Cambridge since 1937, said he was sick of the issue, and when troops began returning from Vietnam he declared the war had been brought to a swifter close through the efforts of peace marchers on university campuses, who were, in his eyes, war heroes.

A Judacus Pernelli Smith had attended Columbia, burned draft cards, plotted to blow up an ROTC building on a neighboring campus, and poured quick-set concrete into the sidewalk flag holders along the parade route the day before Independence Day in 1969, in protest of the war.

He dropped out in 1970, returning to Cambridge to do no more than sponge off his parents and smoke Epsom salts mixed with dried banana peels and nutmeg until his speech was permanently impaired and tremors infiltrated his hands with a life of their own.

Having no one else even close to being worthy of the honor, Russell Calliope Biederbaum showed great pleasure in unveiling the magnificent statue of the long-haired, slouching hippie, disowned by his father but an honored citizen nonetheless.

Still Playing Bass for Weidemeyer

It's nothing new for a rock band to name its act after the leader of the group, like Santana or Van Halen. Not many know that the first group to do such a thing was a band formed in 1965 by Ed Weidemeyer in Gowanda, New York, a small town on the southern periphery of Buffalo.

Ed Weidemeyer was a tax lawyer in his late fifties who sat in with his son Arnold's garage band from time to time. When Arnold succumbed to state fair food poisoning, Ed replaced him as lead guitarist and singer and, using his natural power of persuasion, made it a permanent position.

Not only did he excel at electric guitar, autoharp, and accordion, he wrote his own music and lyrics, none of which was ever any good. But he did have an innate sense of what an audience desired, which, where Weidemeyer was concerned, was lots of breaks and intermissions.

Aside from Ed Weidemeyer himself, who was white-haired and conservative in dress and manner, the members of Weidemeyer (bass player Lance Thumnale, Irv Bippitybam on drums, and Nels "86 Fingers" Aldreck on keyboards) were young, boorish, and unpleasant, with long hair and everything.

They stayed with Weidemeyer only because Gowanda, being a small town, didn't have any other acts to join. "And anyway," said "86 Fingers" Aldreck, who, out of principle, never played the highest or lowest keys on the piano, "a bird in the hand is...ummm..." Too much LSD rendered him incapable of remembering the rest.

Weidemeyer specialized in playing other people's big hits without adding any flair of their own. Their theme song became "Devil With a Blue Dress On," more or less by default. It was the only song they could play from start to finish without a screw-up.

Ed Weidemeyer became locally famous for publicly trying to coax his wife Ruth into donning a blue dress and appearing with the band on stage. "Just walk around up there while we play the song," he'd say to her in restaurants, at the movies, even in church. She was adamant in her refusal, however, being self-conscious of her thinning white hair that was rapidly turning a sickly yellow.

When Lance Thumnale's phone rang one evening while he laboriously worked on an all-bass version of *Bowlegged*

Woman, Knock-Kneed Man, how was he to know it would be his old girlfriend, Olivia Outspot?

"Lance, how are you, and what's new?"

"Still playing bass for Weidemeyer," he said.

"I'm still in love with you, you know," she told him.

She was there at their next concert at the town armory. She even agreed to prance around on stage, but not with a blue dress on; she didn't own one. She wore a dress of red and yellow plaid instead.

"It's the next best thing," Ed groaned into the mike in response to the deafening roar of the crowd.

"Would Not, Want Not"

Norm Billideau made a practice of infuriating his wife, Bertha, by dropping curt, homespun sayings he claimed he remembered his grandfather saying whenever she tried to communicate honestly with him.

"The hen that clucks is the one that laid the egg," he'd say whenever she had a complaint about anything.

"Another pie in the larder left to rot," he'd say when she'd tell him she didn't appreciate another pair of rubber fishing boots for her birthday.

"The man who shits fast don't shit long," he'd say when she compared his income with one of the neighbor's.

But worst of all was his reaction every time she suggested they go out and have a little fun. A movie, a nice dinner, a moonlit walk, no matter what, his answer was always the same: "Would not, want not."

He was more than content to dance with her once a week on the living room carpet to Wayne King's "Waltz Night in Heaven" but Bertha was sick of this, just going through the motions the last several times, though Norm couldn't have cared less.

It was on a Saturday when Bertha packed up and left. “There’s got to be more to life than this,” she sobbed. Norm waved goodbye sadly but said nothing.

Less than two weeks later, Bertha was back. She found that she’d really had it good with Norm. Trouble was, Norm wouldn’t take her back. He found how nice things could be without her.

The Days of Bernard Quaker

I

Bernard Vivian-Louis Quaker was an old, old man, kind-hearted, honest, and respected, but mixed up in many things and ways.

“I’m on my vat to the garage,” he mumbled as he gingerly tiptoed around the sleeping dogs. What he’d meant to say was, “I’m on my way to the bathroom,” for he felt a familiar chest pain and needed his needed medicine.

Upon opening the medicine chest, he cried, “Now where are my cosmetics when I eat them?” meaning, “Now where are my drugs when I need them?” Little did he know that earlier in the afternoon they’d fallen off the shelf and rolled behind the laundry basket.

Bernard Quaker’s chest pains grew worse, forcing him to lie back on the bathroom floor, where he experienced vivid dreams.

II

When Bernard came to, his apartment was on fire.

“Oh, my cat!” he yelled, getting up from the sticky floor,

his heart ailment still in full grip. “Call the Fire Cabbage!” he cried, meaning, “Call the Fire Department!”

“Head!” he screamed, meaning, “Help!”

Suddenly a beam broke loose from the fiery ceiling, crashing down upon Bernard. The next thing he saw was from a bed.

III

Bernard focused his dazzled eyes on the young male doctor.

“Mr. Quaker,” garbled the doctor to Bernard’s swirling ears, “you are lucky to be alive.”

“Thank horseness,” replied the old man, attempting without luck to rise.

“Stay still,” the doctor advised.

“But I have to go to the garage,” Bernard responded.

“That’s all taken care of,” said the doctor.

IV

“I’m glad to be here in my own cream of wheat,” said a tired Bernard Vivian-Louis Quaker, meaning it was good to be home again, despite the fire’s damage. “Too much excitement can make anyone go pots and pans,” he murmured, sitting on the yellow toilet.

Son of a Kooky Linguist

Juxtaposition Henry Alworth was named by his father, Leonardo, a kooky linguist at the local university, a man who liked to tinker and diddle with words. He’d always been amused by the word “juxtaposition” and secretly dreamed of having a son by that name.

His wife, Sylvia, lay in the hospital bed cradling the newborn in her arms and smiling up at her husband, who smiled back down on her like a genuine oaf of a schmuck.

"Little Henry looks just like his father," she said. Leonardo continued to smile, wondering just who she was talking about since the scrawny baby looked nothing like him, but he didn't say anything, not wanting to start an argument.

Weeks ago they'd agreed on the name Henry Alexander Alworth, Henry for Sylvia's father, long dead and remembered through rose-colored glasses, Alexander for her brother, with whom she hadn't spoken in fifteen years due to bent grudges.

Leonardo kissed his wife on the lips and the baby on the crown, then left to officially deliver the papers to the staff at the desk. On the way, temptation got the best of him and he erased the name on the form, replacing it with "Juxtaposition Henry Alworth." With a satisfied smirk, he delivered the papers and returned to his wife and kid.

Sylvia was furious when she learned that her son's name was Juxtaposition and she murdered Leo outright. After serving four years of a life sentence, she was reunited with her son, who she called Juxxie, which in her mind sounded a little more natural and American.

Surprisingly, Juxxie Alworth grew up to be a fairly normal, middle-of-the-road schnook. He became a dentist who received inconsistent reviews from his patients.

On the wall of his office there hung a sign sizing up his entire attitude toward his work: "50/50: Better Than No Chance at All." This was Juxxie's roundabout way of saying there were no guarantees on his work. His main problem was his stubborn insistence not to use modern dental terminology in his notes or directives.

"Filling needed on upper, third from the right," he'd say to his assistant, Miss Lovejoy Lockjaw. "Lower, fifth from the left is rotten and needs to be yanked but quick."

The trouble lay in the fact that Dr. Juxxie Alworth had an annoying mental block as to which was left or right. "Was I standing in front of or behind the patient when I made my diagnosis?"

Business eventually slacked off as the word got out about his shabby technique, but Juxxie Alworth wasn't one to look down in the mouth for long. He made up for his mental lapses with shrewdness.

He found a discarded sign in the trash one morning that read, "All Christmas Items 75% Off." He placed the sign in his window and it increased business temporarily despite it being June, but these kinds of tricks only work for so long.

Juxxie Alworth thought daily of quitting his job, which was a natural reaction to his lack of success. But in spite of his troubles, he loved dentistry. And, like everybody else, he needed the money badly.

"Did you ever consider retiring?" a fellow dentist concerned about the image of dentistry in general once asked Juxxie.

"I don't know if I want to, but I wish I could if I did," he replied in a typically indecisive manner.

Another Distasteful Adventure at the Highview Hotel

Antonio Antonioppio and his small but wonderful family were traveling through the Arkansas Ozark foothills when they spied a sign that intrigued them, mainly because they were dog-tired and were looking for a place to bed down for the night: "Highview Hotel—6 Miles Ahead and Counting"

They all agreed the scenery would be delightful, so they drove on with joyous hearts. Imagine their puzzlement when the road dipped into a valley and continued to descend into a tree-choked wilderness.

Down, down they slid. The air grew dank and the smiles bent themselves into frowns. At last they pulled up to the hotel, situated on the edge of a dismal swamp.

"How do you mean, calling this place the "Highview Hotel?" Antonio Antonioppio demanded.

"Why shouldn't it be?" asked the proprietor.

"My God!" hollered Antonio. "It's in a swamp! How dare you lure people here, calling it the Highview Hotel?"

"My name, sir, is Charles Highview, the hotel has been in my family for ages, and if you'd like to register I can escort you inside at present."

Feeling foolish, Antonio fell in behind Mr. Highview and was about to enter the lobby, when a man in a dark suit appeared out of nowhere, taking him by the elbow and leading him astray.

"I am Scheister Loyyyer," the man said in clipped tones. "I will represent you in a suit of false advertising against the hotel if you wish. My reputation is secure."

Antonio Antonioppio was all ears until he learned the lawyer had a permanent residence at the hotel and made his living preying on people who were suckered there by the sign. He was, in fact, a Highview himself, being a cousin of some sort from a distant marriage. His real name was Leonard Highview, but he'd changed it to Scheister Loyyyer upon passing his bar exam, due to the new truth-in-labeling law. It was all downhill from there.

The Antonioppio family heartily enjoyed their stay at the Highview, especially when during the evening volleyball game Scheister Loyyyer was eaten by a sprightly alligator, who later pled guilty to his cannibalistic ways.

In a Tavern on the Waterfront

Had his beer mug been a little bit bigger, he would have

stuck his head right into it. So drunk he could barely stay on his stool, Sol Hilgenberg moaned and mumbled to himself as he sat in Pete's Jolly Tap in beautiful downtown Columbus.

"I coulda been a Pip," he slurred. "I coulda been a Pip." He vomited into his beer.

Indeed he'd come close. Back in his prime he'd tried out for a position with Gladys Knight and the Pips, remaining a candidate until the bitter end.

"What would have been wrong with having four Pips?" he asked himself for the hundred-thousandth time. Then, in a fit of rare belligerence, he pounded his fist on the bar and growled, "Hell, who's Gladys Knight anyway? It coulda been 'Sol Hilgenberg and the Pips!'"

"Time to go home, buddy," drawled the bartender.

"I coulda been a Pip," wept Sol, his head now planted solidly on the bar. "I coulda been a Pip."

"Y'are a pip," said Hubert Drousnoggin from across the way, a lonely businessman whose latent homosexuality was taking a drunken stroll the way an iceberg bobs at the surface of the ocean.

Putting Vince in His Place

Madge had friends to call and cards to write. Vince had nothing to do and was annoyed with Madge for claiming to be too busy to play croquet with him in the yard.

Madge and Vince were married friends between the ages of forty and fifty. When Vince was annoyed, as he was now with Madge, there was no living with him. Madge was in no mood for his clamor tonight.

She locked him up in a tight box to keep him out of her hair until she was through with her tasks. It felt so good she never let him out.

An Unfortunate Slip of the Tongue

This year's fundraiser for The Home For Fathers Who Can't Keep Their Children's Names Straight (THFFWCKTCNS) was to feature a golf tournament, the big news being that Jack Nicklaus himself had accepted an invitation to take part. In a tearful interview prior to the competition, Nicklaus spilled his guts as to the horror of growing up in a home with a father who would have benefited immensely from THFFWCKTCNS.

"'Tommy, er, Sue, ah, Bobby, uh, Frank, er, JACK!'" the great golfer demonstrated, choking back sobs of shame and humiliation. "It was awful."

To everyone's surprise, Nicklaus had a subpar day and was bested by Ogden Oostboyg, a chump of a fellow from Elbow Rash, just a mile or two up the creek from the golf course.

Most folks would be more than satisfied with beating Jack Nicklaus at golf, but not Ogden Oostboyg. He immediately challenged Nicklaus to a pancake flip-off, Ogden's real specialty.

Having nothing better to do and nowhere else to go, Nicklaus accepted the challenge. People stood around on the edge of their seats as the competition resulted in a tie and had to go into sudden death.

Dusk was upon them and Ogden had to call his wife, Olga, to let her know he'd be a little late. But, being caught up in the excitement, he got confused when she answered the phone and began calling her by the names of his golfing buddies.

"Hello, Herman,um, Al, ah, Joe, um, Gilroy, er, Ned, ah, HONEY!" Before he could get any further, men in white jackets carried him away kicking and screaming.

Olga visited him every Saturday morning at THFFWCKTCNS. "It's not strictly for fathers," she'd tell him in response to his complaints. "Husbands qualify too."

Hardtack and Pemmican

Hardtack and Pemmican, private investigators by trade, sat bored in their office, trying to think of ways to instigate a crime wave, a shoplifting spree, even a traffic snarl, anything to bring some business their way.

"It's hell being a private investigator in a town like this," griped Rudolph Pemmican, former night watchman at an auto plant in Detroit, which qualified him to handle any crime that might occur in Cloverbud, Iowa.

"I wanted to get out of the big city, but this is ridiculous," said Biff Hardtack, retired coach of the St. Louis Cardinals football team. "The mayor is competent, the people are honest and hard-working, the kids are into sports and their studies. Shit."

Last week they thought they had something when Mrs. Lilywhite reported her geranium pots out of place on her back porch. Before they could even dig in, a neighbor kid confessed and rearranged them the way they belonged.

The phone rang occasionally, resulting in the two detectives engaging in a wrestling match to see who got to answer the call. More often than not, it was a wrong number.

The pastor reported his keys stolen last March, but while Hardtack and Pemmican were still putting on their jackets, he called back to say he found them on the hood of his car in the garage.

Even dogs that ran away returned before the investigators could begin their search.

"The hell with this," Biff Hardtack finally said, independently wealthy anyway. He wanted to go home and gaze at his trophies and reminisce about his induction into the NFL Hall of Fame.

"What was your secret, Coach?" a reporter asked after his acceptance speech on that glorious afternoon in 1962.

"Well," Biff said, clearing his throat. "The most important

thing was that I put my second-best players into the starting positions. That way when they got hurt I could replace them with better quality players."

Rudolph Pemmican heard the coach on TV and immediately called to offer him a partnership in his private eye agency.

"I need someone who thinks like you," he said.

Too bad it didn't work out. Pemmican pleaded with Hardtack to reconsider, using all sorts of cliches that usually appeal to coaches. "When the going gets tough, the tough get going." "If it ain't broke, don't fix it." "A journey of a thousand miles begins with a single step." The cliches didn't necessarily fit the situation, but Pemmican wasn't exactly a Baryshnikov when it came to thinking on his feet and he was desperate.

And after all, Biff Hardtack was not just anybody, he was an award-winning football coach who had played in the interior line as a collegian, getting himself battered to a pulp week after week after week. He didn't think like most people.

"I hate those cliches," he said as he walked home along the quiet streets of Cloverbud. "To me, a single step just might lead to a journey of a thousand miles. It's those single steps one ought to try to avoid."

Baby Aerobics with Rusty Innards

Rusty Innards was, at best, a lackluster country and western singer to begin with, but when he started drinking heavily and leaving the stage in mid-concert, or not showing up for scheduled engagements at all, something had to give.

He quit drinking and his life lost the misery so essential to writing proper lyrics to country songs. He realized he was finished.

He did, however, have a name that a sizable portion of the

populace would recognize, for better or worse, and he was determined to capitalize on this fact. He opened a chain of health spas.

Rusty developed a series of exercise videos that assured a lifelong wealth in royalties alone. "Baby Aerobics With Rusty Innards" became more popular than the Jane Fonda workout videos ever dreamed of being.

The video begins with Rusty, eyes dark and glowing clumping back and forth in his rhinestone-studded cowboy boots, beard down to mid-stomach, chatting amicably with a group of pregnant women lounging about the studio on pillows and cushions of various sizes and colors. His speech is littered with endearing country slang and amusing bits of corn pone.

He gets them into position and talks them through the exercises, urging the viewers at home to join in with the mothers on the screen.

"Yer baby'll be healthier'n a two-mule hoss if y'foller these exercises ever' mornin' after breakfiss," he enthuses. "Y'gotta get 'em movin' 'fore dey's born if'n ya wanna have yerself a rip-strappin' son or a lithe 'n limber gal."

He sits back in a beanbag chair and lets his protruding stomach sag out like a roll of gelatinous fat. Sucking it in until it's relatively flat, he starts by letting the top bubble out grotesquely. The bulge rolls downward until the sag settles just above his longhorn steer belt buckle.

"C'mon, ladies," he chortles. "This one I call 'Pig in Mud.' Yer youngun'll feel like a newborn piglet in loose slop. Suck in that tummy and roll those abdom'nals from top t' bottom…"

He goes on to 'Country Corn on the Cob,' 'Frolickin' Foal,' and 'Biscuits 'n Grease.' 'Old Sow Waddle,' in which he exhorts the ladies to make their stomachs roll from side to side "like a sow waddlin' to the trough at feedin' time," was by far the most popular among studio participants and viewers alike.

Due to the success of this revolutionary exercise video, Rusty Innards was able to retire at age thirty-eight. He died at forty-four, much to the dismay of his doctors who told him repeatedly to lose some weight.

But once before Rusty had lost everything due to straightening out his wicked ways. "They's more old drunks than they is old doctors," he gasped on his deathbed. "I shoulda listened to Willie Nelson all along."

The Sigh Heard 'Round the World

Mother's advice rang in Bentley Coynrittern's ears even while he was still in the womb. "I don't want him born premature," Raynilda Coynrittern hollered to her next door neighbor, Gwilgin Funby, as he lay on his back under the car in the driveway struggling to get the crankcase free so he could replace 'the frickin' thing.' "But I certainly don't want him late either."

Bentley arrived on the due date.

All through the pregnancy, Raynilda had resented her husband, Airedale, who lollygagged at work every day while she sat around being pregnant.

She'd finally taken off the 130 pounds she'd gained when *I'm Dickens, He's Fenster* went off the air, making herself attractive again to Airedale, causing a new friskiness in him that led to her getting into this predicament where her figure again bulged out of shape in the wrong places.

And Bentley was made to take the blame, later becoming a problem child, but not in the usual way.

He drove his parents crazy responding promptly to every directive and tending to every household need. Not a smidgen of advice got by him, not a word of scolding fell on deaf ears.

Most young boys hate piano lessons and act as if they're dying when told to forgo the ball game across the street in order to practice. Not Bentley.

He practiced on into the evening, drowning out all the good shows, causing his parents to get cranky prematurely. He took his lessons far more seriously than anyone would have expected. His bedroom walls were covered with portraits of Beethoven, Bach, and Marvin Hamlisch.

When at last they pushed him out the door at age eighteen, Raynilda collapsed onto the davenport with what Airedale later described as "the sigh heard 'round the world." They at last were finished with him and could resume the life they'd been living before he came along, which wasn't much either, but certainly not as grueling as life with Bentley.

Bentley, though gone from the nest, never forgot any of his mother's advice. He worked for a time as an attendant for an ambulance service. His first emergency call involved a motorcycle accident victim who had scraped himself across 120 feet of pavement until his facial features were rearranged haphazardly up and down his chest and stomach.

When the young man was stripped of his clothing in the back of the speeding ambulance, Bentley couldn't contain his shock. "Didn't your mother ever tell you not to wear old and ragged underwear, and for this very reason?" The dying man moaned and rolled away from Bentley's angry face.

Reprimanded later by the boss, Bentley promised not to stick his nose into other people's affairs. But, with how he felt about his mother, it was easier said than done.

Two weeks later, a co-worker overheard him whisper into the ear of a heart attack victim on the way to the hospital, "I hope your underwear is decent!" He was promptly fired, not to be missed.

Eventually, Bentley Coynrittern was hired to replace Denise Ann DeNephew, receptionist for Drs. Wydely Spreddum and Ben Dover, at the Clinic For Internal Disease. For over thirty years, Denise had answered the phones and greeted patients, doling out medical advice and meddling in their concerns, going so far as to read aloud from patient files to those sitting bored in the waiting room.

Bentley had found his place.

The Goldfish of Florian Grenzbidado

Florian Grenzbidado was killed by a moving truck. A crowd gathered, of course, but no one knew him.

Somewhere, tucked away in the vast sea of tenements and highrises, was a small abode that Florian had called home. A goldfish swam in a large bowl by the window in the bedroom.

Just outside the bowl sat a small box of food for the fish, who Florian had named Greg, after a childhood friend.

After an agonizing time of it, Greg died, as starving children in far away countries rooted through garbage piles looking for food.